PUFFIN BOOKS

The New Cut Gang: Thunderbolt's Waxwork

Philip Pullman was born in Norwich in 1946. He was brought up in Africa, Australia, London and Wales, and went to Oxford University to read English. He now lives in Oxford.

Another book by Philip Pullman

THE NEW CUT GANG:
THE GAS-FITTER'S BALL

The NEW CUT GANG

THUNDERBOLT'S WAXWORK

Philip Pullman

Illustrated by Mark Thomas

PUFFIN BOOKS

PUFFIN BOOKS

Published by the Penguin Group
Penguin Books Ltd, 80 Strand, London WC2R 0RL, England
Penguin Putnam Inc., 375 Hudson Street, New York, New York 10014, USA
Penguin Books Australia Ltd, 250 Camberwell Road, Camberwell, Victoria 3124, Australia
Penguin Books Canada Ltd, 10 Alcorn Avenue, Toronto, Ontario, Canada M4V 3B2
Penguin Books India (P) Ltd, 11 Community Centre, Panchsheel Park, New Delhi – 110 017, India
Penguin Books (NZ) Ltd, Cnr Rosedale and Airborne Roads, Albany, Auckland, New Zealand
Penguin Books (South Africa) (Pty) Ltd, 24 Sturdee Avenue, Rosebank 2196, South Africa

Penguin Books Ltd, Registered Offices: 80 Strand, London WC2R 0RL, England

www.penguin.com

Penguin Books Ltd, Registered Offices: Harmondsworth, Middlesex, England

First published by Viking 1994
Published in Puffin Books 1996
8

Text copyright © Philip Pullman, 1994
Illustrations copyright © Mark Thomas, 1994
All rights reserved

The moral right of the author and illustrator has been asserted

Filmset in Plantin light

Made and printed in England by Clays Ltd, St Ives plc

British Library Cataloguing in Publication Data
A CIP catalogue record for this book is available from the British Library

ISBN 0–140–36410–2

Contents

One

Dippy's Ambition

Lambeth, 1894

The criminal career of Thunderbolt Dobney began on a foggy November evening outside the Waxwork Museum. Thunderbolt had never thought of himself as a criminal; he was a mild and scholarly youth. But he was a passionate collector of curiosities, and for some days now he had been filled with desire for the odd-shaped lump of lead belonging to Harry Fitchett, a boy in his class. Finally, after much bargaining, he had persuaded Harry to swap it for a length of catapult rubber.

The exchange took place under the hissing gaslight by the Waxworks entrance.

'This is stolen property, this lead,' said Harry. 'It come off that old statue of King Neptune outside the Lamb and Flag. *You* remember.'

The knowledge that he was holding a piece of criminal history added to Thunderbolt's pride. Harry ran off, twanging his length of rubber at the legs of passers-by, and Thunderbolt dropped the lead into his pocket with a guilty thrill.

The others, meanwhile, were gazing up at the poster advertising the latest attraction at the Waxworks.

'A victim of the Atrocious Death of a Thousand Cuts,' read Benny Kaminsky.

Benny was a stocky, dark-haired boy of eleven. When you saw Benny at first you took him for an ordinary boy. When you'd known him for half an hour you were convinced he was a genius. When you'd known him for a day you suspected he was the Devil, but by then it was too late: you were drawn in. Everyone who knew Benny was drawn in, because he was less like a boy than a whirlpool. The New Cut Gang were proud to follow him.

Thunderbolt peered at the poster Benny was looking at.

'Ah! I read about that in the encyclopedia,' he said. 'What they do is, they tie 'em up and slice bits off 'em with a razor. They start at the feet and work up. Takes *hours*,' he added enthusiastically, pushing his glasses up with a grimy finger.

'Well?' said Bridie. 'Are we going in or not?'

Bridie Malone was red-haired and red-tempered, and at least as fierce as Benny. Everywhere that Bridie went, her little brother Sharky Bob came too. He was a placid and benevolent child who would eat anything, and often did. The others didn't mind having Sharky about because they'd often won bets on his ability to chew up and swallow dog biscuits, champagne corks, fish heads, and anything else the sporting citizens of Lambeth offered him.

He was plucking at Bridie's sleeve now.

'Dippy's selling chestnuts,' he said. 'I seen him just now. I likes chestnuts,' he added helpfully.

So did they all. The Death of a Thousand Cuts forgotten, they streamed across the road and around the corner to Rummage's Emporium, where Dippy

Hitchcock had set up his hot-chestnut stand. Rummage's Emporium took up several shop-fronts. It was the biggest store in Lambeth, and the windows were blazing with light and streaming with condensation. Old Dippy was selling some chestnuts to a customer who'd just come out, and he greeted the kids cheerfully.

'Three penn'orth, please, Dippy,' said Benny.

He had earned a shilling earlier that day by holding some horses for the Peretti Brothers (Removals, Funerals, and Seaside Excursions). You got sixteen chestnuts for a penny, so that would mean twelve each. The kids stood around Dippy's little stove to eat them, fishing the smoking nuts out of the triangular twists of paper and rolling them between their palms to loosen the skin.

'You been in the Waxworks then?' said Dippy. 'I'd like to be a waxwork.'

'They don't make waxworks of hot-chestnut men,' said Thunderbolt. 'Only Kings and criminals and people like that.'

'I used to be a criminal,' said Dippy. 'I set out to be a pickpocket. But I had to give it up on account of me conscience.'

'Unless you're a celebrated murderer, it's not worth mentioning crime,' said Benny. 'Ain't you done anything else to make you famous, Dippy?'

Dippy rubbed his bristly jaw. 'No,' he said mournfully. 'But I'd love to be a waxwork. Make me feel me life had been worthwhile, somehow.'

Another customer came out of Rummage's and bought a pennyworth of chestnuts, paying with a

3

sixpence. Bridie was interested in this waxwork talk, but even more interested in the nearest window, where a stout and shiny man called Mr Paget, the Gentlemen's Outfitting Manager, was clambering about arranging a mannequin. Every time he lifted the arm into position and turned round to pick up some gloves from behind him, the arm fell down again, and he got more and more vexed and more and more shiny. The arm came up – the arm fell down; he dropped the gloves; the dummy swung forward and butted him on the nose; he said (very visibly) a wicked word, and looked guiltily out at the pair of wide blue eyes watching him. Bridie turned at once to a kindly old gentleman passing by and asked him what the word meant, pointing in at Mr Paget.

'No! No!' Mr Paget mouthed in horror, and waved his hands, but then had to lurch sideways to catch the dummy, and knocked over a chair; which was the point when Mr Rummage stormed out of the main entrance.

'Get away from that window!' he bellowed, shaking his fists. 'I will not have vagrants and coster-mongers on my property! I'll have the law on you! Smoking up my windows and leaving your filthy rubbish on the pavement! Get away! Go on! Hook it!'

Dippy didn't want to move, because standing in the bright light of the window among the crowds going in and out of the shop was good for business; but Mr Rummage was a roaring, red-faced bully, and no one could stand up to his shouting for long. So the gang helped Dippy to move and set up a little

4

further away, and Mr Rummage scowled and strutted back inside.

'Great bellowing bag of wind,' said Bridie.

'I'd like to get me *revenge* on him,' scowled Benny.

The gang had taken a dim view of Mr Rummage since the time he'd run them out of the shop for offering to demonstrate the camping equipment. It was Benny's idea. They'd offered to pitch a tent inside the store, and cook meals on a 'Vesuvius' Patent Folding Stove, and filter water with an 'Antibuggo' Microbial Filter, and sleep in the 'Kumfisnooze' Patent Sleeping Valise, and they'd even put on a display of Apache war dancing to entertain the customers. Benny was very proud of this plan. In the way of his plans, this one had soon spun out of control, and he imagined a Corps of Demonstrators, highly skilled and efficiently trained kids, say about ten thousand of them to start with, who'd be paid by grateful shopkeepers throughout the kingdom to show customers how to use the goods on sale. Benny would take a small percentage, say about seventy-five per cent, and within a year he'd be rich, have branches in America, float the company on the Stock Exchange, stand for Parliament, et cetera, et cetera.

Anyway, he was explaining to Mr Rummage how useful it would be when Thunderbolt had that accident with the 'Luxuriosum' Folding Umbrella Tent, and then the Peretti twins got carried away in the 'Pegasus' Self-Propelled Invalid Chair, and Sharky Bob discovered the 'Surprise' Officers' Dried Food Ration Tin, and things got out of control. Mr

Rummage had thrown them all out bodily and forbidden them to enter the store ever again.

'Here, Dippy,' said Benny, 'where's me change?'

'Oh, sorry,' said Dippy. 'You give me a shilling, didn't yer? Here's a threepenny bit and a nice new tanner.'

Benny took it, but looked at it oddly and bit it.

'Here, Dippy,' he said, 'this is snide, this is. Where'd you get it from?'

He held it out. It was new and shiny, and there was Queen Victoria and all the letters around the edge, and there was a toothmark right across Her Majesty's nose.

'It's snide all right,' said Bridie. 'Look, Dippy, it ain't a proper sixpence at all!'

They all crowded close. Dippy took the coin and tested it with his four remaining teeth.

'Yeah, I reckon you're right,' he said, baffled. 'It's a fake, and no error. Wonder who passed that on me? Here, you better have some proper money.'

He didn't have another sixpence, so he gave Benny six ordinary pennies, and looked at the snide sixpence with disgust. Thunderbolt could see something else in his expression, too. A sixpence was a lot of money when you only made two or three shillings a day.

But then an old lady came along and bought some chestnuts for her granddaughter, and then Johnny Hopkins came out of the Welsh Harp wiping his whiskers and bought some too, and the gang said goodbye to Dippy and wandered off.

★

'It's not fair,' Bridie said when they reached the Waxworks. 'Whoever gave Dippy that snide sixpence knew they were cheating.'

'It's not fair not letting him be a waxwork either,' Benny said. 'All them waxworks in the Museum, all they done was murder people and discover America and be Kings and Queens and that. Where's the justice in that? I bet if Dippy was a victim of the Death of a Thousand Cuts they'd put him in all right.'

'There's not enough of Dippy to make a thousand bits,' said Bridie.

Benny scowled at the closed door of the Waxwork Museum.

'We'll get Dippy in there if it's the last thing we do,' he said.

When Benny's expression was set like that, the rest of the gang knew better than to argue with him. The others left him there, frowning Napoleonically, and walked home towards Clayton Terrace.

'I wouldn't mind putting one over that Professor who owns the Waxworks,' said Bridie. 'He slung me and Sharky out last July.'

'I bet I can guess why,' said Thunderbolt.

'Well it was only a little finger off one of the blokes being tortured in the Chamber of Horrors, and he'd lost a lot more than that already. Ye'd hardly notice.'

'What did it taste like, Sharky?'

'Nice,' said Sharky Bob stolidly.

'And the Professor made us pay for it, and I had a

threepenny bit, and he took it all. I bet that's enough for a whole arm.'

They walked on through the gathering mist, which was making the gaslights look like dandelion heads.

'I hope Dippy doesn't get another snide sixpence,' said Thunderbolt.

'Ma got one in the butcher's yesterday,' said Bridie. 'Ye should have heard her cursing. Hey, is that yer Pa down there?'

They were outside Number Fifteen, where Thunderbolt and his Pa lived on the ground floor and Bridie and the rest of her large family lived upstairs. Bridie was peering down into the area, the little space in front of the basement window, where an eerie glow was flickering through the grimy window on to the damp bricks.

'Yeah,' said Thunderbolt. 'He's making something new. I dunno what it is, cause it's a trade secret.'

Mr Dobney was in the novelty and fancy gifts trade. He made candlesticks that looked like dragons, pipe-cleaner-dispensers that looked like dog-kennels, soda-water-bottle-holders that swivelled round on a turntable, and all kinds of ingenious devices. His latest line was a combined glove-holder and dog-whistle, but for some reason there was no demand for them, and they hadn't sold at all. So he'd rented the basement specially and started making a new line, only Thunderbolt wasn't allowed to know what it was. All he did know was that it involved electricity: Pa had lugged a lot of heavy batteries and coils of wire down there, and occasional flashes and electrical humming sounds came out from behind the closed door.

'I better get in,' said Thunderbolt. 'Put his tea on.'

'I likes tea,' said Sharky Bob. 'I likes biscuits, and all.'

'Yeah, Sharky, we know,' said Bridie. 'What ye got for yer tea, then?'

'A couple of herrings,' said Thunderbolt.

'How ye going to cook 'em?'

'Dunno. Boil 'em, I suppose. They're only a kind of kipper, and you boil kippers.'

Bridie shook her head in exasperation. 'I better show ye.'

Thunderbolt had been looking after his Pa for nearly a year now, and Mr Dobney had never complained yet. Thunderbolt felt a bit put out by Bridie's contempt for his cooking, but he let her storm into the kitchen and bang about till she found the frying-pan. She was about to put it on the range when she recoiled, and held it under the lamplight to look more closely.

'What in the world've ye been cooking in this?' she said, picking disgustedly at some tar-like substance on the bottom.

'Toffee, I think,' said Thunderbolt, trying to remember. 'That was when Pa thought of going into the toffee-apple trade, and he was trying to find a cheap way of making toffee. He used fish-oil instead of butter, only it didn't set properly . . .'

Bridie put down the frying-pan and found a

skillet. 'This'll do,' she said. 'Give us the herrings and a knife and find me some salt.'

She slid the knife deftly up and down and scraped out some fascinating strings and blobs of fish-innards. Sharky Bob stopped licking the frying-pan and reached for them automatically, and she slapped his hand away.

'Right, now what ye do is make the skillet hot and scatter it with a big spoon of salt and lay the fishes on it. They're oily enough to sizzle by theirselves without any grease. What're ye reading?'

She laid the herrings where Sharky couldn't reach them, tucked a strand of curly red hair behind her ear, and peered at the open books on the table.

'Me homework,' Thunderbolt explained. 'We got to copy out and learn ten words out the dictionary, together with what they mean.'

'*Aardvark*,' read Bridie. '*An edentate insectivorous quadruped*. Well, that's helpful, I'm sure. *Ambergris: fatty substance of a marmoriform or striated appearance, exuded from the intestines of the sperm whale, and highly esteemed by perfumiers*. Yuchh. *Asbestos: a fine fibrous amphibole of chrysotile, capable of incombustibility* . . . What in the world does all that mean?'

'Oh, we don't have to know what it means. Only what it says.'

'And that's what ye get up to in school? Catch *me* going,' said Bridie, removing the frying-pan from Sharky Bob. 'Come on, Shark, time to go. Bye, Thunderbolt.'

Thunderbolt said goodbye, stirred up the fire and put another few lumps of coal on it, brought the lamp to the table and sat down to finish his home-work.

'Hello, son,' said Mr Dobney, coming after a few minutes. 'Blooming cold down there. Brrr! What's for tea?'

He rubbed his hands and held them out to the fire.

'Herrings,' said Thunderbolt. 'I never knew they had giblets in 'em, like chickens do. Bridie took 'em out and showed me how to cook 'em proper. They'll taste all right this time.'

'Tasted all right to me last time,' said Mr Dobney, sitting in the rocking chair and unfolding the paper.

Thunderbolt loved his Pa, and he knew his Pa loved him, but neither of them would have dreamed of saying so. Instead, Mr Dobney was always nice about his son's cooking, and Thunderbolt always thought his father's latest invention would be the best of all, and there was nothing nicer than sitting by the fire of an evening with the kettle simmering and the brass Buddha gleaming on the mantelshelf and Mr Dobney reading scandal out of the paper while Thunderbolt arranged his Museum.

'See you've cleaned the old frying-pan then,' said Mr Dobney. 'Watcher got there?'

'It's a bit of lead,' said Thunderbolt. 'It came off that statue of King Neptune outside the Lamb and Flag. *You* remember.'

He took down the little brass-bound chest that belonged to his Uncle Sam the sailor, and which contained all the treasures of his Museum: the walrus tooth engraved with a picture of the *Cutty Sark* in little scratchy black lines; a dried sea-horse; several cowrie shells; a genuine bone from the nose of a cannibal chief, which Uncle Sam had won from him in a poker game; a lump of rubbery stuff from the Sargasso Sea, which Thunderbolt thought was probably a dried jellyfish. And then there were Thunderbolt's own discoveries: a halfpenny which had been run over by a tram; a twig off one of the bushes in Battersea Park, which if you held it the right way and squinted a bit looked exactly like a little old man; a broken glass slide from a magic lantern, showing Glamis Castle with what Thunderbolt *knew* was a ghost at one of the windows; and forty-six bits of old-fashioned clay pipe from the Thames mud. When they broke a clay pipe, in the olden days when they used to smoke clay pipes, there was nothing to do with it but throw it away, and most of them ended up in the river.

He laid them all out on the table and noticed that he'd spelt Sargasso wrongly on the card that belonged to the dried jellyfish. He rewrote it carefully and scraped a bit of fluff off the lump, which was looking fairly battered. It was a dull colour, sort of grey, really, with sooty streaks. Some of it came off under his fingernail, and he looked at it dubiously.

'Wossat?' said Pa. 'That's old Sam's petroleum wax, innit?'

'I thought it was a dried jellyfish,' said Thunderbolt.

'No, no, son. That's petroleum wax. He got it

from Trinidad. They have this blooming great lake there made of tar. You can walk on it. Here! That's a thought! Shoes with soles made of tar – they'd be waterproof, wouldn't they? I'll have to look into that. No, that's wax, that is.'

'Wax! Dippy! The Waxworks!'

Thunderbolt jumped up excitedly. Pa looked across the top of his paper in mild astonishment, and Thunderbolt explained about Dippy's ambition.

'Ah, I get it,' said Pa, rolling the heavy lump towards him. 'Make a nice head, this would. Funny colour, mind. Still, Dippy's not a healthy colour hisself . . .'

'We could make a body for it and smuggle it in . . . *Dippy Hitchcock, World-Famous Hot-Chestnut Man.* Pity he's not a murderer really. He'd get in easy, then.'

'You wouldn't have to smuggle the whole thing in,' said Pa. 'Just the head.'

'He can't just be a head! *Dippy Hitchcock, the Famous Hot-Chestnut Disembodied Head!*'

'No, no. Just whip the bonce off Charles II or Admiral Nelson or someone and bung Dippy's nut up there instead.'

Thunderbolt felt doubtful. 'I dunno. I think he ought to be hisself, not masquerading as someone else. Wouldn't be the same somehow . . .'

He rolled the petroleum wax towards him. There must have been four pounds of it – maybe five. Then he saw the newspaper, which Pa had picked up again, and read a little headline off the back.

'*Fraudulent utterance of forged coins* . . . What's that, Pa? That story there.'

'Oh, that? Nothing. Lot of fuss about nothing. Come on, Samuel, put yer stuff away, it's nearly bedtime.'

His Pa had never called him Thunderbolt. In fact he'd only been Thunderbolt since the summer, when he'd knocked out Crusher Watkins from the Lower Marsh Gang. Crusher had said something about Thunderbolt's Ma, and Thunderbolt had flown at him with one colossal blow that knocked him out cold – a thunderbolt. Ever since then he'd lived in mortal dread of meeting Crusher again; but it had been worth it.

Two

Arrest

'That's *exactly* what I was going to suggest,' said Benny next day.

That wasn't quite true. What Benny had really been going to suggest was that the gang set up their own Waxwork Museum to compete with the one in the New Cut. The vision of it was already shimmering in his mind like a gigantic soap bubble: an ornate entrance, queues a mile long, waxworks so real they just about sang and danced. And a Chamber of Horrors that would freeze the blood of a ghoul. In Benny's mind Kaminsky's Royal and National Waxworks expanded to fill a space roughly the size of the Crystal Palace, and it was such a success that they had to take it on a tour of America, and he came back a millionaire, and before long he was Sir Benny – Lord Kaminsky – the Duke of Lambeth ... Were there any princesses he could marry?

But in the meantime all they had was Thunderbolt's lump of petroleum wax, or dried jellyfish, or whatever it was. They were sitting in the loft over Hodgkins's Livery Stables, surrounded by straw and the rich smell of horse, and Thunderbolt was showing them the potential head of Dippy Hitchcock.

'I reckon it's beeswax,' said Bridie.

'That ain't beeswax,' said Benny. His father was a tailor, so he knew. 'Beeswax is hard and yeller. This is petroleum wax, no error. They make candles out of it. Easy to carve, and all . . .' He was busy shaving bits off with his penknife. 'Eyes,' he said. 'What we gonna do for eyes?'

Thunderbolt held out a faded watery-looking blue marble.

'This is about the same colour as Dippy's,' he said.

'What use is one?' said Bridie. 'Though I suppose he could be winking. Or have a patch over it like Lord Nelson.'

'I got a blood alley too,' said Thunderbolt doubtfully, fishing out a large white marble with red streaks.

'That'll do,' said Benny. 'He can have one good 'un, and the other can be bloodshot. We need summing for his whiskers, and all . . .'

Making the waxwork took the best part of a day. Benny hung around his father's workshop and borrowed a suit someone hadn't paid for, Bridie contributed a pair of her Uncle Mike's boots, and Thunderbolt managed to snip some hair off the tail of Jasper, the bad-tempered horse in the stable below.

And while Bridie and Thunderbolt stuffed the suit with straw, stuck a broomstick through for a spine and pummelled it all roughly Dippy-shaped, Benny set to work on the head.

The wax was easy to carve. He excavated two

17

holes for eyes, and put the wax he'd dug out aside to make a nose with. Getting the eyes to look right took a long time, and still he wasn't sure it looked exactly like Dippy, not *exactly*; but then it needed a nose, after all. He reached for the wax he'd taken out, and found it was gone.

He knew where to look. Sharky Bob was licking his lips.

'It might be poison,' Benny said hopefully.

'It's nice,' said Sharky. 'I likes that.'

Benny sighed, dug a lump out of the back of the neck to make a nose with, and carried on. After an hour of squeezing the head and pulling it, of smoothing it and rubbing it and squinting at it through half-closed eyes, of trying to shove horse-hair under its nose for a moustache and bits of broken china into its mouth for teeth, he reckoned it was done.

'There,' he said proudly.

The others clustered round.

'Hmm,' said Bridie. 'He looks as if he's going to puke.'

Benny shut the mouth. At once the head took on the pursed-up expression of someone who's just swallowed a caterpillar.

'He's cross-eyed,' said Thunderbolt. 'He looks as drunk as a fish.'

With a heavy sigh, Benny licked his finger and repositioned the dots of liquorice that he'd stuck on the marbles for pupils.

'I'm still not sure about his gob-box,' said Bridie. 'Dippy's is always hanging open.'

With an even heavier sigh, Benny prised the mouth open again. Now Dippy looked like an apprehensive patient about to undergo a new and untried form of dental surgery.

'That's better,' said Thunderbolt. 'But his eyes . . . I dunno . . .'

'You do it then!' said Benny passionately. 'You're so blooming clever, you show us how his eyes ought to go! I spose you been making eyes all your life! I spose you're an *expert* on eyes! I spose no one knows *anything* about eyes except you! I spose people come from all over the *world* to ask you about eyes! Well, go on then! *You* make 'em look right, since you're the only one as knows how!'

He thrust the sticky head at Thunderbolt, who prodded and scraped and shoved for a minute or two. When he'd finished, the blue eye was gazing at the ceiling with the air of a desperate appeal for help, while the red one leered at the floor like a murderer gloating over his victim.

They all stood back and studied it critically.

'Well . . .' said Bridie.

'It ain't got a body yet, has it?' said Benny impatiently. 'Shove it on the broomstick. Course it don't look right just sitting there like a . . . like a *head*.'

Thunderbolt and Bridie waggled the head to and fro till it was well and truly jammed down on the broomstick.

'Ah!' said Benny, and Bridie said, 'That's more like it!' and Sharky Bob said, 'Cor!'

The others could only nod. It was a masterpiece.

Thunderbolt had been carefully writing a label

for it, with all the words spelled correctly, and now he pinned it to the dummy's coat like a medal:

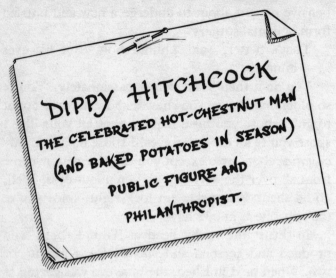

DIPPY HITCHCOCK
THE CELEBRATED HOT-CHESTNUT MAN
(AND BAKED POTATOES IN SEASON)
PUBLIC FIGURE AND
PHILANTHROPIST.

'What's that last word?' said Bridie.

'It means benefactor of mankind,' said Thunderbolt. 'I found it in the dictionary. It's real, all right.'

'Come on then,' said Benny. 'Let's get him to the Museum.'

This was the part of the whole business they'd thought about least. At the back of everyone's mind had been the vague notion that they'd just walk in, set the wax Dippy in a prime position, and walk out again without being seen. But they soon realized that it wasn't going to be that easy.

In fact, the closer they got to the Museum, the more they realized that it wasn't going to be easy at all. For one thing, it cost money to go in, and there

was only enough of Benny's shilling left for two of them.

'It'll have to be me and Bridie,' said Benny. 'Sharky's too little, and Thunderbolt's too clumsy.'

It was true, and Thunderbolt had to admit it; so he and Sharky Bob stood across the road from the entrance of the Museum. It was just getting dark. The first lamps were being lit, and the shop windows on either side of the waxworks glowed bright with their abundance of china plates and hardware, their red and green apothecary's flasks and mahogany drawers of pills. The placard inside the Museum window flickered dimly in the gruesome light shining on it. The proprietor, Professor Dupont, was too canny to put an actual waxwork there, where people could see it free.

Benny and Bridie, carrying the dummy between them with a fine display of casualness, as if it was the sort of thing that everyone took about as a matter of course and they were surprised to see no one else carrying one, dodged across the road between the carts and the omnibuses and ran up the steps to the Museum entrance. There was a little window inside the door where you paid your threepence to the grim lady dressed in black. The tickets were a different colour each day, so you couldn't save yesterday's and go in with that.

They sauntered in, with the dummy's feet bumping on the steps behind them and an inquisitive dog sniffing in their wake. A second or two went by, and Benny and Bridie came out again, in a hurry. In fact, they were running, and no sooner had they skidded to a halt and turned back indignantly than the dummy came hurtling out after them. Bridie caught it neatly, and had to hold it up over the excited dog while Benny shook his fist at the Professor, who took one disdainful look and shut the door.

Thunderbolt and Sharky Bob hadn't even had time to speak.

'Huh,' said Benny with profound scorn. 'Seems to me he doesn't *want* his blooming Waxworks to be successful. Seems to me he wants the same old boring Kings and Queens as every other Waxworks. He's jealous, that's what he is.'

They didn't want to stay there for too long. People were beginning to make unfunny remarks about dummies and Guy Fawkes, and three or four dogs were leaping up and trying to kill it, so the gang trooped crossly back to the stable before going their different ways home.

Thunderbolt was the last to leave. He was feeling fed up. His petroleum wax, and Benny had commandeered it to make the head; his idea in the first place, and he was too clumsy to take the dummy into the Waxworks . . . Nothing was right, somehow. The cold dim light filtering in through the filthy skylight of the stable loft didn't help, and nor did that blooming dummy propped up against a wall. Now he looked at it properly, Thunderbolt thought that he'd never seen anything so horrible.

With a shudder, Thunderbolt closed the trapdoor and climbed down into the stable, avoiding the teeth of old Jasper, to find the stable dog Jezebel whining and scratching at the bottom of the ladder.

'What is it, Jez?' he said.

Jezebel licked his hands with more than her usual friendliness, and howled mournfully. Thunderbolt hurried home through the gathering evening, keeping an eye out for Crusher Watkins and the Lower Marsh Gang.

As he passed the market, he heard Mr Ionides the costermonger shout at a baffled customer: 'Get out of it! Go and pitch yer snide somewhere else!'

More fake sixpences, Thunderbolt thought.

Then from nowhere, and for no reason at all, an idea came into his head. Supposing ... No, he couldn't even put it into words. But the idea wouldn't go away. *Supposing it was Pa doing the coining?*

And once he'd said it to himself it was easier to go on thinking it, though it made him feel hot and heavy, as if he was ill.

Because things had been tight recently. The 'Handi-Cheep' combined glove-holder and dog-whistle had been a failure, and Pa had put a lot into that. And no one seemed to want the self-adjusting pipe-bowl cleaner, and all the 'Eesi-Snip' Smoker's Companions had fallen apart because of a faulty hinge.

And now Pa was busy at something he refused to talk about, even though he and Thunderbolt usually shared everything.

By the time he got as far as that, Thunderbolt had stopped walking altogether. No! The idea was crazy!

(But yesterday when he'd seen the newspaper

article about the forged coins, Pa had folded the paper up hastily and sent him to bed.)

His Pa would never do anything criminal!

(But Uncle Sam had stolen the little brass Buddha on the mantelshelf from a hotel in Rangoon. At least, he'd always claimed he had. And crime ran in families, everyone knew that.)

His family weren't like that.

(But hadn't he, Thunderbolt, become a receiver of stolen property? He was a criminal himself!)

He came to, miserably, outside the butcher's, and remembered what he was going to get for tea. In he went, scuffing up the sawdust, and waited while Mr Graham the butcher parcelled up a leg of pork.

'That's one and sixpence, my love. And a proper sixpence if you please, none of these fancy ones.'

'My neighbour got one in her change yesterday,' said the customer. 'Blooming wicked. How can poor folks live with rotten money going around? Why don't they forge gold sovereigns like what rich people use? Eh?'

When the customer had left, Thunderbolt said, 'A tuppenny pie, please.'

He paid for the pie, and when it was wrapped he said, 'Are there lots of these snide coins about, Mr Graham?'

'They're turning up all over the place, son. All over Lambeth, anyway. *And* shillings and half-crowns. There must be a whole gang of smashers going round.'

Smashers were the people who actually passed

fake coins into circulation. Thunderbolt's heart lifted: Pa wasn't part of a gang, that was certain.

'So one person on their own, like, they couldn't be doing it?'

'One person could be *making* 'em,' said Mr Graham. 'Old Stamper Billings used to work on his own, and he kept going for years.'

'Who?'

'Stamper Billings. *You* remember him, Arthur!' said Mr Graham to a thin old man who'd just come in.

'Old Stamper, yeah, I remember him,' wheezed the old man. 'He turned out all kinds, old Stamper. Course, they caught him in the end – the year Sefton won the Derby. He had a regular crew of smashers. They used to come down from the West End, Soho, and from East as far as Limehouse. That's where he was clever, see. He never uttered 'em round here, so folks was less inclined to peach on him. There's always a nose near by; you don't last long in that trade. But old Stamper lasted longer'n most.'

'Uttered means passed,' said Mr Graham. 'That's the legal term for it. They got him for uttering.'

'Have you taken any of the snide ones, Mr Graham?' said Thunderbolt.

'Yeah, worse luck. D'you want 'em? They're no good to me.'

The butcher fished into the pocket of his apron and brought out three coins.

'Don't you try to spend 'em, now,' he said.

'No! I don't want to spend them. I'm going to put them in my Museum.'

Thunderbolt took the pie to the bakery to be heated. He could think of nothing but the forged coins, and when the pie was in the oven he asked Mr Solomons the baker if *he'd* taken any counterfeit coins.

'No, I'm too fly,' said Mr Solomons. 'They won't get any of them things past me.'

'What do they do to forgers when they catch them?'

'They hang 'em, me boy. It's a capital crime, defacing Her Majesty the Queen. Making false coins is as bad as treason.'

Thunderbolt gulped. 'Do you know how they make fake coins, Mr Solomons?'

The baker looked around, saw there was no one near by, and leaned over the floury wooden counter of the shop to speak confidentially.

'I heard,' he said, 'from a cousin of mine who's a policeman, that they make a plaster-of-Paris mould off a real new coin, and melt some cheap metal and pour it in. Then to make it look like silver they get a bath of spirits of salt and cyanide, cause that's got silver in it, and dip the coins in that and pass an electric current through with a wire from a battery. That makes a bit of silver stick to the coin. There's a craft in it, see.'

Thunderbolt could hardly hear; there was a kind of roaring in his ears. Those electric batteries in the cellar – that wire . . .

He took the fragrant steaming pie when it was

ready and hurried across the road towards home. Then he slowed down. He hurried again; he came to a halt; he didn't know whether to run or stand still.

Finally, heavily, he dragged his steps in through the front door. There was a glow from the area window, like yesterday. And that sharp faint smell: was that spirits of salt? What did they smell like? What *were* spirits of salt?

Thunderbolt took the pie into the kitchen and lit the lamp.

Then he thought: I *must* go and see what he's doing.

He went out into the scullery at the back, where there was a dark little staircase that led down.

And when he got to the bottom of the stairs, he heard voices. Pa was talking to someone.

'I should take 'em up West,' he was saying. 'Try Oxford Street. Lambeth's no good any more. Or you could try up Whiteley's in Queensway . . .'

The other voice said something, and then the outer door closed. Then there were the sounds of tools being put away, and a swishing sound as his father swept the floor, whistling heartlessly. Thunderbolt crept up the stairs again and washed his hands under the pump in the yard, and splashed some water on his face, too, in case his eyes were red.

He stoked the range and put the pie on the table, but that was as far as he got towards making the tea; because just then, as his father came along the hall, there was a loud banging at the front door.

Thunderbolt's heart leapt with fear. He heard Pa's footsteps halt and then turn towards the door;

he heard the handle turn; he heard a loud official voice say:

'Frederick William Dobney?'

'Yus, that's me,' said Pa mildly.

'Frederick William Dobney, I am arresting you on the charge of – '

'NO!'

Thunderbolt flung the kitchen door open and hurled himself down the hall. There was a fat policeman at the door, with a thin one beside him, and there was Pa, looking baffled. The thin policeman made a grab for Thunderbolt before he got to Pa, and held him back. He was too strong. As hard as Thunderbolt struggled, he couldn't break free.

'Pa! Pa!' he shouted desperately, but the other policeman had the handcuffs on his father already, and Pa couldn't move.

'Let me talk to my boy!' Pa was saying, but the fat policeman wouldn't, so Pa shouted, 'Let go! Let me talk to him! You can't take me away like this – what's *he* going to do? Sam! Sammy! Don't . . .'

But Thunderbolt didn't hear any more, because the fat policeman was bundling Pa into a closed wagon, and the driver was shaking the reins. Thunderbolt watched with helpless horror as the police wagon trundled away, taking his father with it.

Then there came a great roaring Irish voice from behind, and the clatter of a dozen pairs of feet on the stairs.

'What the divil are ye holding the boy for, ye whey-faced beanstick? Let him go this minute, or I'll take yer helmet and ram it up yer nose!'

Mrs Malone bore down on the policeman like a force of nature. Lightning seemed to play around her head. The policeman took a deep breath to try and speak in his defence, and in the same moment Thunderbolt twisted out of his grasp and hurled himself down the steps into the road, and away.

Three

Into Action

'Thunderbolt?'

Bridie's head looked up through the trapdoor. She called again, softly, and held the little candle-lantern higher.

'Ah, there ye are . . .'

He lay curled up in the furthest corner. His eyes were closed. She clambered in and shut the trap behind her.

'Hey! Wake up, look, I've brought yer pie. Ye must be famished.'

She set the lantern down on an upturned orange-box and unfolded the dirty cloth she'd carried the pie in. Thunderbolt was still pretending to be asleep, and shivering with cold, the poor spalpeen, she thought.

She nudged him with her foot.

'Hey! Thunderbolt! It's only me. The coppers have all gone. Wake up, ye old fool.'

Thunderbolt yawned and pretended to wake up elaborately. He fumbled for his glasses and put them on before opening his eyes.

'Oh. Wotcher, Bridie . . .'

'I brought yer pie.'

'That was for Pa's tea.'

'They'll give him some nosh where he's gone. Eat up or I will.'

'Share it then.'

She cut it in two with her pocket knife and gave him the larger piece.

'What did they nab him for?' she asked.

'Counterfeiting,' he said. In fact he didn't say it clearly at all; his voice shook and she could hardly hear him. Then she worked out what he'd said.

'Ye mean coining? They think *he's* doing it? Begod! That's crazy!'

She laughed loudly enough to make Jasper shift his feet down below. Thunderbolt said nothing; he sat looking down, stolidly chewing the pie.

'Listen, Thunderbolt,' she said, shaking his arm, 'they'll have to let yer Pa go as soon as they find out he never done it. It's a mistake! Yer Pa's no snide-pitcher. Anyway, ye can't stay here. Supposing they lets him out, and he goes home and finds ye gone, and the fire's out and there's no food or nothing?'

Then it was his turn to shrug. And something in the hopeless, unhappy look of him made her suddenly understand why he'd run away.

'Well, anyway,' she said after a moment, 'pile the hay over ye, that'll keep ye warm. I won't leave the lantern, cause ye're a clumsy divil at the best of times and ye'd set the place alight. Ye've got old Dippy there for company – he's better than a watch-dog, if ye ask me. One squint at him and the boldest murderer'd take to his heels. And ye've got half a pie inside ye, so ye won't starve till breakfast time. Go to sleep now, and I'll bring ye a can of milk in the morning.'

'You won't tell anyone I'm here?' he muttered.

'Ye mean Ma? Sure I won't. If she knew where ye were she'd have ye out by the ear and upstairs with us lot in half a shake. Ye're better off out of it. But I'll tell Benny and the others. This is a gang matter now.'

Next morning was cold and damp. The gang should have been at school, but most of them regarded the School Board as the slow-witted opponent in a delightful game, and played hookey at the slightest opportunity. Bridie intercepted Benny on his way out of his father's tailor's shop.

He was outraged when he heard what had happened. Bridie had to thump him before he'd calm down and listen.

'Will ye stow yer noise! Of course the man's innocent and someone else is passing the fakes, but Thunderbolt thinks his father's *guilty*!'

Benny stopped at once. They were on the corner of Crowquill Walk and Hopton Street, at the edge of Lower Marsh territory, and Crusher Watkins and two of his pals were ambling along schoolwards on the other side of the road. They yelled out some coarse remark, but Benny didn't even hear it.

'He *what*?'

'I could tell. Cause Mr Dobney *could* be the forger, see. He's got all the right bits and pieces in that basement, and he knows all about metalwork and so on.'

'I don't believe it,' said Benny. 'And nor should Thunderbolt. Let's go and –'

'There's no point in saying what he should or shouldn't believe,' Bridie said impatiently. 'Poor feller, he's only got his Pa. He thinks the world of his Pa. If he can't trust him any more . . .'

Benny was a passionate, generous boy, and he saw what Bridie meant.

'Right,' he said. 'Right, I'm angry now. We gotta get some *justice*. We gotta do some *detecting*.'

Only the previous summer, Benny had done a job for Mr Sexton Blake, the great detective. It had only been a matter of taking a message to someone and bringing back the reply, but Mr Blake had given him half a crown and told him he was a sharp lad. For the next two weeks, the gang made life a misery for every adult in the New Cut, detecting like frenzy; until they saw the Texas Cowboy Lasso Artists at the Music Hall, anyway, and took to rope-twirling instead. But that detecting had been kids' stuff. This was real.

'First go off,' said Benny, 'we'll go and see Dippy . . .'

They tracked him down at the market, where he was buying a sack of chestnuts.

'How'd you get on at the Waxworks? Am I on display yet?' he said.

'Not quite,' said Benny. 'Listen, Dippy – you still got that snide sixpence?'

'Yeah. Got it here somewhere . . .' The old man fumbled in his waistcoat pocket.

'I'll give yer a ha'penny for it,' said Benny. 'This is evidence, this is.'

The old man was pleased to make something out of the deal, and then the costermonger near by said, 'I've got one, and all. Want to buy that?'

Before long Benny had two more snide sixpences and a snide shilling, and then he ran out of money to buy them with.

'When they catch the geezer as done 'em,' the costermonger said, 'they oughter chop his head orf. Taking money out of people's mouths! If it was good enough for Charles I, it'd be good enough for him.'

'We'll see about that,' said Benny.

Half an hour later, the whole gang was sitting around the orange-box in the stable loft. Bridie had brought a can of milk for Thunderbolt, as she'd promised, and Benny contributed a bagel, and Sharky Bob offered a second-hand humbug, which was so extraordinarily generous that Thunderbolt felt he had to accept.

'Right,' said Benny. 'First we got to examine the evidence.'

He hauled out the coins he'd acquired, which had become jumbled up in his pocket with the rest of the debris there: a piece of chalk, a magnet with several nails stuck to it, a box of Lucifer matches, another box containing a peculiar worm which hadn't moved for several days, a genuine Jezail bullet, a bit of mirror with the edges bound with sticky tape for looking round corners with, a badly scratched lens for examining footprints and bloodstains and lighting fires, and a ragged handkerchief the colour of mud.

He laid the coins out in a row – all shiny, all extremely real-looking, and each of them somewhere marked with a tooth-bite, showing that they were made of soft metal and not proper silver.

'The first clue,' he said, 'is that they all come

from round here. From Dippy and the market, mostly.'

'And I got some from the butcher,' said Thunderbolt. He said it without thinking, and then realized that he might be incriminating his father, but it was too late. 'He told me about Stamper Billings.'

'Who?' said Bridie.

'He was a snide-pitcher,' said Thunderbolt. 'He lived round the New Cut a long time ago.'

'His stuff might be around somewhere still,' said Benny. 'His tools and that. We oughter find out where he lived. And then we oughter find out where these 'uns are being put in circulation. We know there's a lot round here, but is there any round Lower Marsh? Or further off like the Elephant and Castle or Lambeth Walk? Cause they might not be coming from here at all. So what we gotta do is spread out all round Lambeth and find out where there's been snide coins uttered. Only don't say uttered. There's no point using words if you have to explain what they mean each time you say 'em. Just find out how far it goes, and then come back and we'll work out where the centre of it all is.'

'Then what?' said Bridie.

'Then we'll *know*, of course! And we'll be able to clear Thunderbolt's Pa.'

Thunderbolt had become very red. He looked down at the dusty floor and poked a wisp of straw through a crack in the boards.

'Right,' said Bridie. 'We'll do that. Me and Sharky'll go down the Elephant.'

'I likes Elephant,' said Sharky Bob.

'You ain't never ate an elephant!' said Bridie.

'I bet he could,' said Benny. 'And we'll get the rest of the gang to help, and all. We'll get the Peretti twins and – '

'No!' said Thunderbolt desperately.

Bridie shook her head, and Benny said, 'No, maybe not. So you and Sharky's going down the Elephant, and I'll do up Waterloo. And Thunderbolt can do round Lime Tree Walk, and we'll all meet back here at four o'clock . . .'

He and Bridie and Sharky Bob swarmed down the ladder and hurried off in their different directions. Thunderbolt went more slowly. He was reluctant to go into the street, because he felt that everyone who looked at him would know that he was the son of a felon. And such a mean felony! If it had been a grand, swash-buckling felony, like piracy on the high seas, it wouldn't have been so bad. But counterfeiting sixpences was a low, sneaking, snivelling sort of crime, and it only hurt poor people, too. Thunderbolt felt bleak with misery.

And when he tried to stop thinking about Pa, the only other thing that came to mind was his lump of stolen lead, and that only made him imagine that every policeman he saw was after him personally. The lump of lead expanded in his mind to the size of the Rock of Gibraltar, and it was all covered in flags and posters saying, 'Thunderbolt did it! This way! Clayton Terrace, Number Fifteen! The criminal Dobneys again!'

So he did his detecting glumly, and when he met

the others back in the New Cut as the lamps were being lit, he felt entirely worthless.

But Bridie was carrying a couple of bags of Dippy's chestnuts, and Benny had a big stone jug of ginger beer, and Sharky Bob was clutching a bag of apples, and they all looked so full of glee that he began to cheer up. Seeing Benny eating one of the apples, he began to feel hungry too.

But before he could say anything, Benny suddenly pointed down the street and said, 'Wuph! Thumwhun's thtealing Dthippy!'

Wiping apple off his glasses, Thunderbolt looked where Benny was pointing. Someone – a little skinny man in a rat-catcher's cap – was sneaking out of the stableyard gate, and trying unsuccessfully to conceal what he was carrying: the waxwork dummy, Benny's masterpiece, the portrait of Dippy Hitchcock.

'Oy! Stop thief! Come back!'

The little man looked over his shoulder in alarm. Seeing four determined children charging towards him, he gave a yelp and tried to run. But the dummy's dangling legs got between his feet and tripped him up, and as he rolled over on the muddy pavement, squealing with panic, the dummy's flailing arms wrapped themselves around him, so that it looked as if he were being attacked by a monster from a nightmare.

Passers-by stopped to gape. Hearing the shouts, people looked across from the market stalls, came to the door of the Rose and Crown, opened windows and stared. A group of idle layabout dogs appeared from nowhere to surround the thief and the dummy,

barking with joy, just like children round a fight in the playground. An elderly cab-horse shied nervously.

The little man struggled free just as the gang arrived, scrambled to his feet, and fled. Benny was all for chasing him and making a citizen's arrest, but Bridie held him back.

'Never mind him,' she said, 'we still got the dummy.'

'Not all of it,' said Thunderbolt, lifting it up out of reach of the dogs. At some stage its nose had come off, and a terrier called Ron was eating it gleefully. When they realized what he'd got, the other dogs wanted some too, and Ron took the nose and fled; and less than a minute after it had started, all the excitement was over. Carrying the dummy between them, the gang went back into the stable yard, indignant at the dishonesty of adults.

'Shockin',' said Bridie. 'I'm really disturbed.'

'Oughter hang him, at least,' said Benny. 'You can't trust anyone.'

He tenderly removed the dummy's head, smoothing over the edges where the nose had come off, shoving the blood-alley back into its socket, removing bits of grit and mud from the cheeks.

'He musta been one of these art thieves,' he said. 'They pinch pictures and statues and fancy china and stuff. Then they flog it to museums or rich Americans. Bound to be an art thief.'

Bridie was last in. She was watching the curious behaviour of a foreign-looking man who'd seen the escape of the thief and the rescue of the dummy. He was peering closely at the ground where the thief had fallen over, and bending down to pick up something too small to see before putting it in an envelope and tucking it securely in his waistcoat pocket.

H'mm, she thought, and followed the others in.

'He looks better without his hooter,' she said, examining the damage. 'More friendly.'

'What you talking about?' said Benny. 'He looks horrible. He looks as if he's been attacked by a lion. How'd you like it if your nose was et off?'

'It wasn't a lion, anyway, it was only old Ron from the fish shop,' said Thunderbolt. 'He don't look too bad. Dig a lump out the back of his neck to make another schnozz and cover the hole with his cap. He's just a bit dusty, that's all.'

Slightly repaired, the dummy was propped up in his usual spot near the skylight, and the gang settled down around the orange-box. The candle-lantern glowed on the apples and the chestnuts as they were divided and devoured, as the ginger beer went the rounds and was emptied, and then Bridie gave Sharky a giant humbug to keep him quiet, and they began to report.

'I went up Blackfriars Bridge way and across the river,' Thunderbolt said. 'There's hardly any over the other side, but lots on this. And then I went down Lime Tree Walk and I got talking to this old beggarman, and he told me about snide-pitching. It's not making the coins that's hard – it's passing them out. He said you need lots of people, cause one bloke can't go into a shop or a pub with a bag full of new coins, it'd look suspicious. So they buy the tanners and shillings for a penny each, and go off and pass 'em out in lots of different places. He gave me a tanner what he'd been given. He thought there was some snide-pitching going on, cause normally he only gets ha'pence and farthings.'

He found his voice getting quieter and quieter. He wanted to help the gang in their detecting, but he might only be helping convict his father. What he really wanted to do was shut his eyes and hide in the dark for ever.

But Bridie was impatient to talk.

'They been getting snide coins down St George's Road and London Road,' she said, 'and one or two at the Elephant, but none down Newington Butts. Nor the New Kent Road. Nor Walworth Road.'

'D'you get any?' said Benny.

'We got three.' She tipped them out of her sticky hand and into Benny's. He looked at them closely before putting them with the rest on the orange-box. '*And*,' she went on triumphantly, 'we talked to Snake-Eyes Melmott the bookie, and he told us where Stamper Billings lived! Guess what? He lived just off the Cut, under where Rummage's is now!'

'Under it?' said Thunderbolt.

'He had a basement. Most coiners work on the top floor of a house, Snake-Eyes told us, cause then they can hear the coppers coming and they got time to sling everything in the fire. But Stamper worked in a basement in a row of houses where Rummage's Emporium is. Old Rummage bought up the whole row.'

Thunderbolt was listening as if his life depended

on it. If most coiners worked on the top floor . . . And Pa was working in the basement . . . But Stamper Billings had worked in a basement, after all.

Benny, meanwhile, could hardly sit still. He was bursting to tell them what he'd found out.

'I've been to Grover and Cohen's in Peacock Alley,' he said. 'Them detectives – *you* remember.'

Grover and Cohen were two extremely dingy private detectives (not in the Sexton Blake class by any means) for whom Benny did occasional jobs. It turned out that he'd spent the afternoon with them, learning about snide-pitching in general and this outbreak in particular.

'But they didn't know much,' he said. 'Course, I had to promise to do a job for 'em. They got to find an old lady's cat what's done a bunk. But I know where to find plenty of cats, that won't take long. Oh, and I got half a dozen snideys this morning down Lambeth Walk.'

He fished them out and put them with the others on the orange-box. He was fizzing and twitching with excitement, so Thunderbolt knew that something else was coming.

'And,' Benny said, 'I solved the crime!'

They looked at him blankly.

'It's true! I solved it!'

He couldn't restrain himself from getting up and doing a little jig like Paddy Phelan the Spoon Dancer. Sharky Bob joined in, shouting with glee.

'He's got a mouse in his drawers,' said Bridie. Then she hit him. 'Stow it, ye half-wit! Sit down and tell us, if ye're such a Sexton Blake!'

43

So Benny stopped and said, 'All right. All right. When did Stamper Billings get caught?'

'Ages ago!' said Bridie.

'It was the year – the year . . .' Thunderbolt hit his head, trying to remember what the butcher had said. 'It was the year Sefton won the Derby!'

'1878,' said Bridie at once.

'Look at the coins!' said Benny. 'Look at the date on 'em!'

A moment's stillness, and then three hands reached out to the pile of shiny silver coins.

'1878!'

'*All* of 'em?'

'It's true!'

'They are! They're all Stamper's!'

'It wasn't Thunderbolt's Pa at all!'

'But . . .'

The *but* was Thunderbolt's, and then he began to believe it. Feverishly he turned all the coins over, and they all looked new, and they all had the date 1878 firmly in the right place. He felt a great bubble of joy rising in his chest, and it nearly became a sob, but he made it into a hiccup, and turned the coins over and over, letting them fall from one hand to the other like dazzling water.

'We can prove he's innocent now!' Benny was saying.

For a moment the others clapped and cheered; but then Bridie said, 'No we can't,' and they fell quiet. She went on, 'This doesn't *prove* anything about Mr Dobney, does it? All it proves is that whoever made 'em used a new 1878 coin to make his mould from.'

'But who'd do that, in 1894?' said Thunderbolt desperately. '1878 coins is sixteen years old. They're bound to be worn a bit. These 'uns *must've* been made back then.'

'And anyway, if Stamper Billings did make 'em, why've they only started turning up now?' said Bridie.

'Cause where did Stamper live?' Benny demanded. 'Under Rummage's, that's where! What I reckon is, Stamper made hundreds of these snideys, and hid 'em, and they was never found. Then Rummage bought the place and turned it into a big shop, and found the loot in the basement or in a secret hole in the wall or summing. And it's been *him* passing 'em out.'

'But Mr Rummage is rich,' said Thunderbolt. 'What'd he want to pass out snide tanners for?'

'Cause he's mean as well as rich,' said Benny. 'We *know* he is. And he's got the perfect place to do it! In a big shop like that, what's always busy, it'd be dead easy to slip a dodgy tanner in someone's change. And we know that Rummage's is dead plum smack in the middle of the area they're going round in. The further from Rummage's, the less there are. We just proved that today.'

'It could be . . .' said Bridie. 'And the first time *we* saw one it was just outside Rummage's. I bet someone had just got it in their change and paid Dippy with it.'

'*And* they opened that new department in Rummage's basement last month!' Thunderbolt remembered. 'He could have found Stamper's coins when they did the alterations.'

'*And* he's a scurvy miserable old git,' said Benny. 'It's bound to be him.'

Mr Rummage certainly *was* a scurvy miserable old git. He was famous for it. The gang had been excluded from the Emporium after that unfortunate business in the Camping Department, but Mr Rummage didn't only exclude helpful people like them; he excluded all sorts, grown-ups as well. He got the taste for it soon after he had an electric lift fitted in the shop, one of the first in London. He had an attendant standing by on each floor with smelling-salts and brandy in case the customers felt faint after this new experience. Naturally the lifts were soon crowded with customers pretending to stagger out fainting, and Mr Rummage lost his temper and excluded them. Then there was old Molly Tomkins. She was mad, but perfectly harmless. She fell in love with one of the window dummies and wanted to climb in the window to be with him. The poor old soul thought Mr Rummage had taken him prisoner. She was excluded even from walking up and down the pavement outside the window, and she used to stand across the road and signal to the dummy until they came to take her away to Bedlam.

So Rummage was a bad-tempered bully; and now he was passing out snide coins as well, or so it seemed. Thunderbolt thought of his Pa, locked in a cell. He could almost feel his thoughts beating at the prison bars like a carrier pigeon with a message of hope.

'We'll have to *get* him!' Benny said. 'We'll have to catch him red-handed.'

'But how?' said Bridie. 'He won't let us in the shop! Why don't we just go and tell the police?'

It seemed the obvious thing to do, but Thunderbolt felt a drizzle of fear at the very thought. He'd forgotten about his *own* crime for a few moments.

'Maybe,' he said wildly, 'maybe we ought to get in the shop and find the hiding-place.'

'That wouldn't take long, would it?' said Bridie. 'There's only twenty-two departments, after all. And only about ten thousand places to hide things in each one. We could probably do it in about ten minutes.'

'Well –' Thunderbolt began, but Benny held up his hand and said, 'Sssh.'

They all fell still.

Benny tiptoed over to the trapdoor and crouched to listen. Then he looked up. 'There's someone down there,' he whispered.

A spy!

They looked at one another, with a nameless thrill shivering its way up their backs. Silently each of them picked up a weapon – a catapult, a bit of stick, a clasp knife, anything that came to hand – and resolved to sell themselves dearly.

Jasper was moving about restlessly below. And then into the stillness came a creak. It was a familiar creak: it was the sound the fifteenth rung of the ladder made. The intruder was nearly at the top.

Thunderbolt, Bridie, and Benny tiptoed in utter silence to the trapdoor. Sharky Bob scowled fiercely from the orange-box. A draught from somewhere made the flame in the little lantern quiver, and the shadows flapped around the loft like great dark flags.

Beneath the trapdoor they could hear a scratching, scrabbling sound as the intruder fumbled for the bolt.

He was muttering, too, and in a foreign language. Thunderbolt thought it might be French. He made out the words, *'Morbleu! Que diable ont-ils fait avec le . . . Ah! Voilà . . .'*

The bolt slid open.

The trapdoor lifted.

And there in the guttering lantern-light was the face of a stranger. He had a little pointed beard and a neat pearl-grey hat and kid gloves, and whatever he expected to see, it wasn't a ring of fierce faces glaring down, an array of dangerous weapons all pointed at him. He gave a startled gasp.

'Non! Non! Aah –'

The fifteenth step could cope with the kids' weight, but the Frenchman was plump and well-fed, and when he suddenly stepped down on to the cracked rung it gave way completely.

'Waaaah!' he cried as he vanished.

That's the same in French as it is in English, Thunderbolt thought, interested.

The kids all crowded to the rim of the hole and peered through. They knew it wouldn't have pleased old Jasper to have Frenchmen falling among his feet like hailstones, and a shrill whinny and a loud stamping confirmed it. More shouts of alarm in a mixture of French and panic followed, and then the spy found the stable door and fled.

The gang looked at one another. Benny shook his head.

'An escaped lunatic,' he said. 'I spect they'll catch him soon. Or maybe he was another art thief . . . Yeah, he looked like an art thief. Bound to be. But never mind him. *I* know how to catch Rummage red-handed. Close the lid and I'll tell you my plan . . .'

Four

The Transformation of Dippy Hitchcock

'Slummin',' said Benny sagely, once they were all seated round the orange-box again. 'We gotta get Rummage slummin'.'

'Eh?' said Bridie.

'Slummin'. Grover and Cohen told me about it. See, the trouble with snide coins is they look too new. If they was *real* silver tanners they'd look more battered. So he's gotta think that passing 'em out like this is dangerous, and he oughter make 'em look older by slummin' 'em. You make up a mixture of lampblack and oil and rub it in, and there they are, slummed. See? So he gets the idea that he's gotta do this, and so he does it, and we goes in and catches him red-handed.'

'Oh,' said Thunderbolt.

'I see,' said Bridie.

'How we going to make him do it in the first place?' said Thunderbolt.

'We get Dippy to go in and talk about it so Rummage overhears.'

'Dippy's been excluded,' Bridie pointed out.

'All right, someone else then! Grover or Cohen or someone. Or your uncles,' he said to Bridie.

'Well, yes, but how are *we* going to get in?' she said.

'And how are we going to prove it?' said Thunderbolt.

'I'll borrow Grover and Cohen's detective camera and take a pitcher of him doing it.'

Bridie looked doubtful.

'They won't –' said Bridie.

'Sposing –' said Thunderbolt.

'I don't think –' said Bridie.

'What if –' said Thunderbolt.

Benny lost his temper.

'You don't *deserve* me!' he stormed. 'You deserve someone like Crusher Watkins tellin' you what to do! You deserve that bloomin' *dummy* leadin' you! I'm *wasted* here. You got no more daring nor imagination than a cupboard full of beetles! This is a plan what even Sexton Blake'd be proud of. In fact I think I'll go and work for him full time, stead of leadin' you. I think I'll be his partner. I think he'd appreciate me. He'd say he wished *he* could think of plans like that. *Yes but! Sposing! What if!*'

'I was just going to say,' said Thunderbolt, 'what if we got Dippy to let us in?'

There was a silence. Thunderbolt was sitting forward and blinking hard, the way he did when he was thinking, and he dabbed up his spectacles and tried to explain the idea that was wobbling in his mind like a soap-bubble.

'It's my lead,' he said breathlessly, 'my bit of lead what I bought from Harry Fitchett, what came off the statue on the horse-trough – and it was Dippy wanting to be a waxwork – and it was the man in the window, that other day, when Dippy got his first snide tanner –'

'What you *talking* about?' said Benny.

Thunderbolt explained. The summer before, the Metropolitan Horse-Trough and Drinking Fountain Association had made the mistake of setting up a fine lead statue of King Neptune by the horse-trough just across the road from J. Beazley the scrap-metal dealer's. This was too tempting for the local citizens to resist, with lead fetching the price it did, and thirty-six hours after the statue was unveiled it had vanished for good. Unrecognizable lumps of lead kept turning up at Beazley's yard for weeks afterwards; in fact it was one of those very lumps which was causing Thunderbolt such spasms of criminal guilt.

But once the plinth was empty, the drinkers at the Lamb and Flag nearby felt it needed occupying, so one warm evening they each got up in turn and posed for the admiration and criticism of the general public. Tommy Glossop's Napoleon had been highly praised, and Mrs Amelia Price's Lady Macbeth had pleased the connoisseurs of the drama; but Dippy Hitchcock's Moses Parting the Red Sea had drawn gasps of admiration and a round of applause. Dippy had struck a dramatic attitude and held it for so long that you'd have thought the rest of him was made of wood as well as his head, as Mrs Fanny Blodgett of the Excelsior Coffee Rooms put it. The Peretti twins had won two shillings betting on him.

'Ahh!' said Benny, with a sigh of profound satisfaction. 'I'm beginning to get it.'

'Well, tell *me* then!' said Bridie.

'We get Dippy dressed posh,' said Thunderbolt, 'and clean him up a bit, and he goes and stands in the window like a dummy till closing time, and then he lets us in.'

Bridie began to grin. Benny was already grinning.

'It's a stunner!' he said. 'It's a corker!'

'It's the best one yet!' said Bridie.

And Thunderbolt began to think that things might not be so bad after all. They agreed to catch Dippy and put the plan into action next day; no point in hanging around, as Bridie said.

When they left the hideout, Thunderbolt lingered behind. Bridie said, 'Come on home, Thunderbolt.'

He twisted his lip. 'I dunno,' he said.

'We're on the right track now! Ye can sleep in yer own bed, and Ma'll give ye a feed – you can't stay here another night.'

'Well . . .'

He looked back at the dummy. It looked so forlorn and abandoned that he felt almost bound to stay and keep it company.

Bridie saw where he was looking.

'Yeah,' she said, 'I got a funny feeling about that. I reckon we ought to hide it. That thief knew where it was, and I reckon the Frenchman was after it as well, and he knows where to come now.'

'The escaped lunatic? He won't come back after a trampling from Jasper.'

'All the same, I reckon we oughter take it with us. Ye never know.'

'You never know,' said Sharky solemnly.

So they covered the wax head with an old nosebag of Jasper's, crammed the floppy limbs together and bound them tightly with a bit of twine that Thunderbolt kept round his waist as an emergency belt or climbing rope or lasso, and then manoeuvred the unwieldy bundle through the trapdoor and down the ladder, homewards.

It was strange being home again. And not at all nice; the grate was cold and full of ash, there was no oil for the lamp, and only a bit of stale bread to eat. Thunderbolt was on the point of feeling very sorry for himself indeed when Bridie came down and invited him upstairs.

'Ma says if ye don't come and have a bite of supper she'll box yer ears,' she told him, so he had no choice.

The Malones' kitchen was full of five different kinds of noise and three different kinds of smoke. Mrs Malone was shouting, Sharky Bob was banging two spoons together, Uncle Paddy was playing a tin whistle, Mary and the two middle girls were arguing over a board game called Wibbly Wob, and a frying-pan of potatoes was hissing and bubbling on the range. The three kinds of smoke came from the frying-pan, the fire, and Uncle Mikey's pipe.

'Here's the champion!' said Uncle Paddy, who'd seen the famous fight with Crusher Watkins.

'Have they let yer Da out yet?' said Mary.

'Course they haven't, else he'd've come home, wouldn't he?' snapped Bridie.

Mrs Malone turned her broad scarlet face to Thunderbolt.

'What d'ye think ye're doing skulking in a stable all night, gossoon?' she roared.

'I thought they'd arrest me as well,' Thunderbolt explained.

'Let 'em try!' she bellowed. 'Bridie! Dishes!'

She brought the frying-pan to the table, and a tide of Malones came in: from the floor, from under chairs, from under the table itself. The smaller ones perched on the big ones' knees, the uncles had a couple apiece, and Thunderbolt shared his chair with Sharky Bob.

'Mind yer bacon with Sharky!' said someone. 'Gobble it quick else he'll have it.'

Mrs Malone dished out the fried potatoes, and Uncle Paddy cut slices off a vast slab of boiled bacon. For a short while they all stopped talking. The only sound was the clatter of cutlery and the munching of a dozen full mouths.

Then there was a satisfied sigh, and then another, and Uncle Paddy said, 'That was a fine piece of bacon, Michael.'

'A happy pig, Patrick,' said Uncle Mikey, and Thunderbolt saw a secret wink pass between them.

Mrs Malone cleared the bacon away and sliced up some bread and treacle for everyone, and then Bridie washed the dishes. Thunderbolt wondered when she was going to broach the subject of Benny's plan, but she knew her uncles; she waited until they'd got their pipes going and the kids were playing around their feet.

When she'd done the dishes she said, 'Uncle Mikey? Can ye do us a favour?'

Uncle Mikey didn't live there; he was visiting from Limehouse, where his barque was unloading.

'As long as it's tomorrow. We're back off to the Baltic Sea the day after. What d'ye want me to do?'

'You and Uncle Paddy both. Ye've got to go into Rummage's, and walk around till you see Mr Rummage himself. Then ye've got to mention snide money and see if he pricks up his ears. If he comes close and listens, ye've got to talk about slummin'.'

'What the divil's that, then?' said Uncle Paddy.

'Hush, Patrick; this is a prime lark,' said Uncle Mikey. 'Carry on, girl.'

'One of ye's got to tell the other that what professionals do with new snide coins is to rub a mixture of lampblack and oil into 'em, to make 'em look used. Otherwise they look too new and people get suspicious. Just make sure old Rummage hears that and then walk away casual-like. See?'

Uncle Mikey raised his ginger eyebrows and directed a long stream of smoke at the ceiling.

'I can't imagine what this is all about, but I wouldn't mind playing a trick on that great swaggering gomus,' he said. 'What d'ye say, Paddy?'

'Well, why not?' said Uncle Patrick.

And Thunderbolt felt as pleased as if both uncles belonged to him.

Next morning he intended to find Dippy at once, but unfortunately the school attendance officer was standing in the street with his little black notebook, and there was no escaping him. At playtime, Thunderbolt had a brief and almost absent-minded fight with a boy who said that Mr Dobney would certainly be hanged, and then Thunderbolt would have to go to the orphanage; and once he'd successfully mended his glasses with a piece of string from his emergency lasso, he settled down resignedly to learning the principal rivers of England and Wales. The drone of the master – the sniffing and scratching and fidgeting of the other kids – the stuffy fug that always developed when a lot of dirty bodies shared a closed space with a big iron stove – it all enveloped him with gloom.

As he trudged out of the BOYS gateway at four o'clock, he heard Benny yell 'Thunderbolt!' from across the street and saw him jumping up and down with impatience, beckoning him frantically.

He darted across.

'They done it!' Benny said. 'Bridie's uncles! They went in looking like a pair of swells, and they waited till Rummage was *this* far away, and when they started talking about snide money he jumped so much he nearly snapped his suspenders!'

Thunderbolt's gloom began to lift. 'The trouble is I ain't had time to find Dippy,' he said. 'The attendance officer nabbed us and I couldn't escape.'

'Oh, blimey. He could be anywhere. If we don't get him in there tonight we're sunk!'

'I been wondering how to tell him anyway.'

'Me too. I suppose the twins might know where he is . . .'

The Peretti twins, Angela and Zerlina, were a year or two younger than the others. They had attached themselves to the New Cut Gang some time ago, and for all Benny's scorn of kids (apart from Sharky Bob) he had a healthy respect for their sharp wits, not to mention their ferocity. You wouldn't think they were fierce to look at them; they looked like little Italian angels, with big innocent brown eyes and masses of black curly hair; but when they were roused, they were worse than African Sam, whose temper was legendary.

And more to the point, Dippy was fond of them. They might be able to persuade him even if the boys couldn't.

'Yeah,' said Thunderbolt. 'Good idea.'

The two boys set off like greyhounds. They found the twins arguing with Snake-Eyes Melmott the bookie outside the Welsh Harp, dragged them away, and told them the whole story in fifty seconds flat.

'Right!' said Angela. 'We'll find him.'

'We'll make him do it if it's the last thing he does,' said Zerlina.

They raced up and down the New Cut, and along Lower Marsh, and saw a hot-pea man and a muffin-man and a pie-man, but no Dippy. Then they charged up one side of Waterloo Road as far as the railway bridge and down the other as far as St George's Circus, and then back up again, and finally they ran into him coming out of Chippin's the greengrocer's on the corner of Webber Row.

'Dippy! Listen –'

'Dippy, you got to do summing for us –'

'You gotta be a public benefactor!'

'It's heroic, Dippy, and only you can do it!'

Dippy blinked at them suspiciously.

'Wot?' he said.

'It's easy, honest,' said Thunderbolt, tugging his sleeve.

'I'll push yer stove for yer, Dippy,' said Benny.

Dippy feebly allowed the twins to lead him along the crowded pavement behind his hot stove.

'But . . .' he said.

'There's nothing to it, Dip,' said Angela. 'It's not as if we're asking you to shin up a drainpipe or crawl through a sewer –'

'Or get shot at or stabbed –' said Zerlina.

'Or hanged, or poisoned,' said Benny. 'Or suffer the Death of a Thousand Cuts, like that bloke in the Waxworks.'

They didn't stop talking until they reached Clayton Terrace. They parked Dippy's stove in the backyard and went into Thunderbolt's kitchen, where Bridie was waiting by the light of a candle with scissors and flour and rouge and a jar of dripping.

'Woss this all about then?' said Dippy, profoundly suspicious. 'Woss that dripping for?'

'Yer hair, of course!' said Bridie. 'It won't lie flat on its own, and we can't afford proper macassar oil. Now sit down and –'

He goggled.

'Me *hair*?'

'And the flour's for yer cheeks – no! Don't let him run away! Sit down, Dippy. Do as ye're told!'

Since she had a pair of scissors in her hand, and since she was her mother's daughter, he sat down at once. The twins held him down while she worked on him. Benny, meanwhile, was taking a suit out of a bag. He'd borrowed it from his father's workshop, since the customer it was being altered for had to go away rather suddenly for his health, so he obviously didn't want it. Benny shook it out with practised hands, swung it this way and that to admire the nap of the cloth, and brushed a fleck or two of dust from the black shoulders.

While he was doing that, Thunderbolt polished his father's best pair of boots. Mr Dobney had great big feet, so Dippy was bound to be comfortable in them.

'You're going to look like the Duke of Clarence,' said Benny admiringly.

'I hope not,' said Dippy. 'He's dead.'

'Well, before he was dead. Nice schmutter, this. Look at the cut, eh!'

'I wish I knew what you was doing,' Dippy mumbled.

Thunderbolt stopped polishing to gaze at the change Bridie was working on Dippy's face. His moustache – a great ragged thing like the back end of a dirty dog – was trim and tidy; his grimy all-weather complexion had been whitened to the colour of plaster-of-Paris with the flour and then given a healthy pink glow with the rouge, and his straggly grey hair was pasted flat with the dripping.

'H'mm,' said Bridie, her head on one side.

'He looks . . . distinguished,' said Angela.

'He looks embalmed,' said Zerlina.

'I know what it is!' said Bridie suddenly. 'It's his barnet.'

'Not more dripping?' said Dippy helplessly.

But Sharky Bob was scraping out the dripping

pot: there was none left. Anyway, that wasn't what Bridie had in mind.

'It's too grey,' she said. 'Ye look shockin' old with grey hair.'

'I *am* shockin' old!'

'Yeah, but that won't do tonight. Ye gotta look young and fit and healthy. Give us that boot-polish, Thunderbolt . . .'

· 'But why? Why?' Dippy gave a groan and closed his eyes.

Taking no notice, she opened the tin of blacking. With the help of a table-knife she spread the sticky black substance on Dippy's hair, smoothing it artistically and running the back of the knife-blade along the parting.

When that was done, they made him stand up and got the suit on his nerveless limbs, and then made him step into Mr Dobney's boots. Then Angela adjusted the celluloid collar and Zerlina tied the tasteful lime-green and violet cravat.

They all gazed in awe. A shiny, porcelain-like glaze covered Dippy's features; the boot-polish and the dripping had combined into a glistening, varnished, jet-black sheet over the top of his head.

'Miraculous,' said Benny. 'You're a star, Dippy.' Three or four money-making schemes darted like hummingbirds through the tropical jungle of Benny's brain, but he ignored them; there'd be plenty more. 'Listen, we couldn't have picked a better night for it. That Mr Paget's been rearranging the windows. They'll never notice!'

The old man's eyes rolled from one to the other

of them. His cheeks were too stiffly pasted for him to speak easily, but a flicker of alarm showed in his bloodshot eyes.

'Winders?' he said. 'What winders?'

'Oh, yeah,' said Benny. 'We better tell you the rest of the plan. Sit down, Dip, old boy. Thunderbolt, guard the door . . .'

'Oh no! No! Absolutely not!'

'Oh yes! You *got* to!'

'I refuse!'

'You can't, you promised!'

'I never promised –'

'He did, didn't he? Didn't he promise?'

'Dippy, this is a matter of public honour!'

'It's a matter of shame and humiliation, you mean! Me stand in Rummage's window? Like a ruddy mannequin? Oh, no. Oh, no. Never in a thousand years. You must be stark raving . . . Well, you *are*, I know you are, all of yer, imps of Satan, tormentin' me! Get thee behind me! Help!'

'Dippy,' said Bridie sternly, 'if ye don't do as ye're told I swear I'll think up a hideous vengeance.'

'Cut his livers out,' suggested Angela.

'He's only got one,' said Zerlina. 'You're thinking of kidneys.'

'Them and all. Cut 'em out and hang 'em on his hot-chestnut stove. That'd teach him a lesson.'

Dippy groaned and tottered.

'I don't believe what's happenin',' he muttered. 'This must be an evil vision brought on by drink. I'll never touch it again, I swear . . .'

'No, it ain't, Dippy, and you're no drunkard,' said Bridie urgently. 'It's real. So listen, you old clot. You got a job to do.'

Dippy's eyes swivelled pleadingly from one to another of them and found no mercy. Even Sharky Bob was feeling the edge of his spoon as if it was a dagger, and frowning like a buccaneer.

'Oh, all right,' Dippy muttered. 'I know when I'm beat.'

They all sat down. Thunderbolt stayed near the door in case Dippy made a run for it, and Benny looked at the old tin clock on the mantelpiece.

'What's the time? Six o'clock? That's good. We got two hours before Rummage's closes. Now listen, Dippy. You know these snide coins? Well, a feller called Stamper Billings made 'em sixteen years ago and hid 'em in the basement where Rummage's is now. And Rummage found 'em and he passes 'em out in the change, and no one knows except us, and we're gonna catch him. So we made him think he oughter make the coins look old else he'll be found out, and he's gonna do it tonight ... And we got a secret weapon. Look!'

And he produced, with a flourish, the detective camera that belonged to Messrs Grover and Cohen, and which had taken him half an hour's solid pestering to borrow. It was a flat circular object bound in dark leather. You wore it hanging on your chest with the lens poking out through a buttonhole on your waistcoat, and you exposed each picture by pulling a ring at the bottom.

'Now listen, Dippy,' he went on, 'we gotta get in

64

and photograph Rummage with those coins, but we can't hide in the shop and wait cause he won't let us in in the first place. So we need someone in there first to unbolt the door and let us in. So –'

'Catch him!' said Bridie, and the twins each seized a leg as Dippy made for the window.

There was a brief struggle, in the course of which the candle was knocked over. It went out at once.

'Got him?' said Benny. 'Sit him down, then. Thunderbolt, where's the matches?'

'I only got one match left.'

'We'll just have to sit in the dark, then,' said Benny. 'Dippy? You listening?'

An inarticulate moan made its way out of Dippy's lips.

'Good. Cause it's gotta be *you* what hides in there and –'

'Sssh!'

It was Bridie, and she laid a strong hand on Benny's arm to emphasize the message.

'What's that noise outside?' she whispered.

Everyone fell still. In the yard outside the kitchen window someone was whispering, and then there came the unmistakable sound of fingernails on the window-frame, feeling for the way in.

Then there was a cracking, splintered sound followed by a whispered, 'You sure this is the right house?'

The other man whispered back, 'Yeah. It's right under that noisy old trot Mary Malone.'

Thunderbolt heard a soft intake of breath from

Bridie. Benny made a signal, and all the kids sank to hide in a crouch behind the table and the rocking-chair. In the dim light through the oilcloth blind Thunderbolt could see Dippy, still sitting in his chair in a trance of fear, like a rabbit mesmerized by a snake.

'And you're sure they brung it here?' said the first voice.

'I seen 'em! The kid with the glasses had it under his arm . . .'

They're talking about the dummy! Thunderbolt thought in astonishment, and from the wide eyes gleaming beside him, he saw that the others were equally surprised. And then there was a soft tinkling sound as glass fell to the floor, and the oilcloth blind was raised cautiously.

Crouching very still, the kids saw two heads outlined against the sky. Then one man struck a match and lit a bull's-eye lantern. The smell of hot oil drifted into the room, and then a ray of light shone out full on the still figure of Dippy.

'That's it!' came a hoarse whisper.

'You sure?'

'Yeah! Horrible ugly thing. I'd know it anywhere. Get in quick and stuff it in the –'

But Thunderbolt could hold back no longer. Invading his home! Planning to steal his property! Normally he was sure he was the most timid person in the whole of Lambeth, but out of somewhere a great rage burst up in him, and he yelled with fury and leapt at the burglar.

And then there was confusion. Finding the darkness inhabited by several imps or demons with whirl-ing fists and savage teeth (Sharky having connected with a leg) instead of a placid wax dummy, the invaders shouted in horrible terror and scrambled towards the open window. A hideous clatter of pots and pans – devilish yells and roars – the rip of the oilcloth tearing from top to bottom – the crash of the upturned table; and then both men were in the yard, bleating with fear, and leaping over the wall and making off down the alley.

Windows were flung open all around, and faces peered down curiously.

'Bridie!' came a mighty roar from above, and the kids, picking themselves up off the damp stones of the yard or leaning out of the kitchen window, saw the huge form of Mrs Malone looking down, sur-rounded by clouds of steamy light. 'What the divil's going on?'

'Burglars, Ma,' Bridie called up cheerfully. 'We chased 'em off.'

'I'm glad to hear it. Where's the boy?'

'Hello!' shouted Sharky Bob. 'I et a leg, Ma!'

'Let's hope it wasn't poisoned,' said Mrs Malone, and banged the window shut.

The kids clambered back to find Dippy rigid with fear. He slowly opened one eye.

'They gorn?' he whispered.

'That's the third time someone's been after that dummy,' said Bridie.

'There's more to this than meets the eye,' said Angela.

'Never mind that now,' said Benny impatiently.

'We better get Dippy over to Rummage's and settled in that window.'

Thunderbolt looked around the kitchen and twisted his lips at the damage. A broken window, a torn blind, and the big saucepan had a dent that wasn't there before; but there was something more worrying than that.

'Listen,' he said to no one in particular, 'those blokes must've been tipped off.'

'Probably more art collectors,' said Benny impatiently. 'Probably going to put it in a private museum. But never mind that now. Come on, else Rummage's 'll be closing.'

'No! *Listen!*' said Thunderbolt. 'What do they want the dummy *for*? I reckon they're gonna try the same trick! I reckon they know we're on Rummage's trail!'

'I bet they don't,' said Bridie. 'No one knows that.'

'Come *on!*' said Benny, fizzing with impatience.

He tugged Dippy's arm. The twins followed, but Thunderbolt hung back; he was still puzzled about this interest in the dummy.

And so was Bridie.

'That French geezer, that monsewer in the stable,' she said, 'he didn't look like a burgular. I don't think he's connected with this last lot at all. And the first bloke that took it – I'll swear that was Sid the Swede. These blokes were different.'

'It's a mystery,' said Thunderbolt. 'I reckon it's as much of a mystery as –'

'Oh! I nearly forgot!' she said, fishing a little

metal flask out of her pocket. 'Take this, and give Dippy a drop if he comes over faint. It's Uncle Paddy's horse-reviver. He gave it to old Charlie Maggott's mare when she wouldn't run.'

'But aren't you coming?'

'I just want to have another look at the dummy. I'll come on after.'

Before he left, Thunderbolt reached up to his museum and took out his lump of criminal lead. He hardly knew why he was doing it: he had the vague idea that he could drop it in the gutter and pretend it had nothing to do with him.

'Come *on*, Thunderbolt!' said Angela, coming back to drag at his arm.

'Yeah, I'm coming . . .'

They caught up with the others at the end of Herriot Street, just around the corner from Rummage's. Dippy had a bowler hat pulled down so low, and a muffler pulled up so high, that all you could see between them were two watery eyes and a pointy, white, glistening nose that looked as if it would break off if it knocked against anything. He was shuffling along in Mr Dobney's boots, unable to lift his feet because he left the boots behind when he did.

'You must have really little feet, Dippy,' said Angela. 'Like a chest of drawers or summing.'

'Never mind his trotter-boxes,' said Benny. 'Once he gets in that window he can take 'em off if he wants to. I wouldn't be surprised if Rummage's gonna close a bit earlier tonight. I bet he's anxious. I bet he's consumed by guilt. I bet he feels shockin' nervous.'

Dippy had begun to tremble. Thunderbolt saw his knees shaking in the tight trousers, and then he heard a clicking sound, which was Dippy's four teeth going.

'What's he doing? He's not *shivering*? You can't have a shivering dummy, it'd give the game away at once!' said Benny, disconcerted.

'He better have some of this,' said Thunderbolt.

'Eh? Wossat?' said Dippy.

'It's Bridie's Uncle Paddy's horse-reviver,' explained Thunderbolt. 'I should think one good swig'd set you up for an hour, at least.'

Dippy inserted the flask between the muffler and the hat-brim. There was a brief sucking noise and then a gasp.

'Nice, Dippy?' said Zerlina.

He couldn't speak. 'Ah – ah –' he murmured faintly, and handed back the flask. Benny took a sniff at it and made a face. But whatever it had done for Charlie Maggott's mare, the horse-reviver had certainly fortified Dippy. He shuffled bravely forward, head held high in order to see under the hat-brim.

They stopped by the bright gaslit windows of the big store, where crowds of customers struggled to get through the crowds coming out. Thunderbolt felt a rush of anger: here was Mr Rummage, making all the money he must be making, and still he was so mean that he couldn't resist passing out snide coins and having another man punished for it.

'Do yer best, Dippy!' he said.

'You got that horse-reviver?' Dippy muttered.

'Give him the flask,' said Angela.

Thunderbolt passed it over.

'D'you think that's a good idea?' said Zerlina.

'It's only a little flask,' said Benny. 'It's good for him, I expect. It smells horrible so it's bound to be.'

They saw the sense of that, all having experienced medicines of uncommon vileness in their time.

'Good luck, Dippy!' said Thunderbolt.

And Dippy put the flask in his pocket and shuffled forward into the great shop. No King or Queen had ever felt more proud of their army on the way to battle than the New Cut Gang felt of Dippy Hitchcock then, as he weaved uncertainly through the crowds and into the very jaws of danger.

Five

Hiccups, Wasps, and Straw

Dippy Hitchcock had led a peaceful, unambitious life up till then. The most dangerous thing that had ever happened to him was nearly getting knocked over by a sheep. That had been early one morning, when he was visiting his cousin Ted in Newbury, and a flock of sheep being driven to market had come up the road at a fast gallop. A particularly savage old ewe had made for Dippy as if intending to trample him to death, and he'd skipped out of the way just in time. Apart from that he'd led a placid life.

So going into Rummage's on a daring mission like this was making his poor old heart skip about like a grasshopper. The further in he went, the more he felt the need for another nip of horse-reviver. Perhaps when he was in the window . . .

But getting in the window wasn't going to be easy. It looked simple enough from outside – there was a little door at the back of the window-space that obviously led into the shop; but what you couldn't see from the street was that the little doors opened behind the counters. He'd have to get behind a counter first, and there was a swarm of shop-assistants already there, who'd be bound to think it odd if a strange wax-like figure clambered over to join them. It wasn't the sort of thing you'd miss.

Then there was the problem of which window to pick. There were six of them, and to the best of Dippy's recollection, only one of them showed men's clothing. Of the others, one displayed china dinner services, another bicycles, another bamboo furniture, and the last two displayed ladies' wear. The thought of finding himself in the window with the ladies' nightclothes made Dippy break out into a cold sweat. This was very unfortunate, because the sweat combined with the flour on his face to make a sort of gluey porridge which slowly seeped downwards, making him look as if he was melting. People who saw him shuddered and said, 'Poor man.'

So which window should it be? The most likely one was the one whose little door opened behind the Gentlemen's Outfitting. However, presiding over the other side of the counter was the man Benny and the gang had seen arranging the window on the evening they got the first coin: Mr Paget the Gentlemen's Outfitting Manager. He'd fixed a suspicious eye on Dippy the second the old man had come into view. In his experience, people with that many clothes on only intended to hide things in them, and if ever he'd seen a shoplifter, it was this shady-looking individual in the big boots.

Then Mr Paget blinked, peered more closely, and found his suspicions confirmed. The wretch was wearing a mask!

The staff at Rummage's were always being urged to look out for shoplifters, and Mr Rummage even offered a Thieftaker's Bonus to any assistant who caught one in the act. Mr Paget felt every nerve in his body twitch with the prospect of earning the Thieftaker's Bonus. He snapped his fingers to summon his assistant from the other end of the counter, where he'd been putting away some gloves.

'Leave them gloves and take charge of the counter, Wilkins,' he said. 'I shall only be a few minutes.'

He lifted the wooden flap and stepped through, moving, as he thought, with the caution of a jungle cat. His eyes never left Dippy for a moment. He began to track the old man from department to department, as Dippy blundered blearily from the Gentlemen's Outfitting to the Haberdashery to the Soft Furnishings, and back again, occasionally bouncing gently off the nearest fitting, and every so often stopping to refresh himself with the horse-reviver. Mr Paget, eyes gleaming, moustache bristling, teeth bared like a tiger's, followed him at a short distance, moving in a silent prowl and darting for concealment from place to place.

This might have gone on until the shop closed, but two things happened. Firstly a customer loudly demanded to see some gloves, so Mr Paget's assistant had to leave that part of the counter and attend to him at the other end.

Secondly, another customer tapped Mr Paget on the shoulder when he was being particularly tiger-like behind a delicately balanced display of glass-ware.

Mr Paget leapt like a dog discovered eating from the cat's bowl. His arm nudged the top shelf of the glassware display, and a cascade of crystal decanters, salt-cellars, goblets and tumblers fell to the floor

74

with a mighty crash. Mr Paget gave a yelp of dismay, and tried simultaneously to pick up the broken glass, answer the customer's question, and keep an eye on Dippy; but he couldn't do all three, and Dippy was gone.

By now, Dippy had applied so much of the horse-reviver that he was more or less oblivious to falling glassware. Finding himself in the Gentlemen's Outfitting yet again, and seeing the counter unmanned, he vaguely remembered that he had something to do through that little door on the other side.

He clambered over the counter, fell heavily behind it, got up cheerfully, opened the wooden door and was through in a moment.

He found himself in a curious narrow space lit by hissing gaslights, occupied by four or five men standing or sitting very stiffly and wearing smart clothes. There was a big glass wall a couple of feet away, through which he could dimly see crowds of people passing to and fro, and that and the other men in there put him in mind of something.

'Here,' he said to the man standing closest, 'is this the Waxworks?'

The man didn't speak.

'Oy,' said Dippy, and prodded him.

The man fell over.

Dippy thought he'd killed him. He was horrified.

'Sorry!' he gasped. 'I didn't mean to kill yer! Here – have a nip of horse-reviver . . .'

He struggled past the man seated near by and offered the flask to the dead man. Suddenly a suspicion struck him.

'Here,' he said, 'you're a wossname, ain't yer!'

He flicked the man's nose. A hollow knocking sound came from it.

'Ahh,' said Dippy. 'Thassit. I member now. I'm a dummy. Well, you stay there, mate, out the way, and I'll take yer plate. Tape yer place. That.'

He stood up cautiously. No one seemed to have noticed. The other men in the little space were obviously pretending to be dummies as well.

'Not a word, eh?' said Dippy to the nearest one, and winked. 'Prime lark, this is. Gissa bit o' room . . .'

He nudged the man slightly, and he fell over too. Dippy shook his head sadly.

'Drunk,' he said to himself. 'Shockin'.'

He had another nip of the horse-reviver. There didn't seem to be much left. Still, the chair was vacant now, and he could sit down.

He was vaguely aware that there were people watching – that in fact a small crowd was gathering outside the glass. Normally he'd have felt shy, but being a waxwork (he'd forgotten the shop-window plan, and his mind had wandered back to the Waxworks) he didn't feel shy at all. In fact, he thought, I've got quite a talent for this business.

He arranged himself comfortably, legs elegantly crossed, hands on hips, and gazed out at the crowd. He couldn't see them very well. All he could really see was a reflection of himself, and very fine I look too, he thought. He raised his head a little, tilted his chin to one side, loosened the fit of the jacket over his shoulders, and settled into a trance-like stillness.

Outside, P.C. Jellicoe the local constable was urging the crowd to move on.

'Make way there! Come on, move along! Clear the way! Clear the way!'

They protested, but P.C. Jellicoe took no notice. Lot of nonsense! Perfectly ordinary shop-window display. Rather stylish, if anything, but not worth gathering a crowd for.

'Move along! Move along!'

The crowd dispersed reluctantly.

Benny, Thunderbolt and the twins, watching from across the street, sighed with relief as the crowd moved away.

'He's done it!' said Benny. 'That's the first problem out of the way.'

'He's gotta stay there for a long time yet,' said Zerlina doubtfully. 'And people keep looking at him . . . Are they going to leave the window lights on all night?'

'Dunno. What's that little boy staring at?'

For a small boy was tugging at his mother's hand just outside Dippy's window.

'Mummy! Mummy! Look at that dummy! It's got hiccups!' he said in a piercing voice that reached across the street.

'Oh Septimus, *really* . . .' said the mother, stopping reluctantly.

Benny and Thunderbolt listened apprehensively and sidled across the street to see what was going on. Two urchins, who'd seen the nauseating Septimus in his sailor-suit and had come up intent on mayhem, were staring at Dippy instead.

'Cor! Look at him!'

'Must be a mechanical one . . .'

Dippy, legs crossed elegantly, eyes happily vacant, was sitting perfectly still; except that every ten seconds or so his body jerked as if an electric current had been applied to the chair. Soon the urchins, and the sailor-suited Septimus, were counting and joining in.

'Nine – ten – HIC!'

'That was a good 'un! He'll fall over in a minute!'

'Eight – nine – HIC!'

'I heard that one through the glass!'

'How'd they do it?'

'I reckon compressed air.'

'HIC!'

'Or hydraulics. Betcher there's a tube going up his trolleywags –'

'HIC!'

'Septimus, come *on*! This is not the way to behave!'

'Mummy, what are trolleywags?'

'That's *enough*!'

Benny and Thunderbolt exchanged an uneasy glance. Further down the street, P.C. Jellicoe had seen the crowd beginning to form again, and was strolling majestically back to disperse it for the second time. Since that was the last thing they wanted, Benny took the initiative by whipping the caps off the two urchins' heads and running across the street.

'Oy!'

'Oo done that?'

'There he goes –'

'Get 'im!'

Hiccups forgotten, the urchins gave chase. Benny led them along the New Cut and left into Waterloo Road, where he chucked the caps into the back of a dustcart that happened to be passing. There was a brisk exchange of threats and insults, and the urchins raced off after their caps; so that was one problem dealt with.

There were plenty more to come.

Mr Paget was dealing with a problem at that very moment inside the shop. In his excitement after knocking over the glassware and losing Dippy, he rushed about challenging everyone who looked remotely like him. He'd challenged three men in black overcoats and insisted on prodding the face of one of them because he said it looked like a mask; and the customer had made such a fuss that Mr Rummage himself had to come and sort it out.

'I have never been so insulted!' the customer was bellowing.

'I am truly sorry,' Mr Paget kept saying, squirming and bowing and trying to escape by walking backwards. 'I deeply and humbly beg your pardon, but the fact is that your face does look as if –'

'*What?* How dare you? How dare you, sir?' the customer demanded.

Mr Paget squirmed and cringed even more, and backed into a dummy advertising 'Dux-Bak' rainwear, sending it crashing to the floor.

Mr Rummage merely looked at him and raised his eyebrows. When he did that he looked terrifying.

'Well?' he said.

'Yes! I'll pick it up! Sorry! Sorry!'

Mr Paget gathered the 'Dux-Bak' dummy in his arms and laid it on the counter like a corpse in a funeral parlour.

'I'll mend it!' he babbled, sweating at the thought of all the damage he'd done. 'I'll stay behind and mend it personally myself on my own without any help!'

'You've done quite enough damage already,' said Mr Rummage, who had his own reasons for not wanting anyone on the premises after closing time. 'Go! Go on! Leave!'

Mortified, Mr Paget slunk away and left.

By now it was time to close. Mr Rummage ushered out the rest of the staff and went over the whole shop, locking doors and windows, peering suspiciously into cupboards, cloakrooms, lifts, into every corner that might have concealed an intruder or a policeman.

Finally he went to check the main doors again, and had a nasty shock, because peering through the glass at him were four pairs of eyes.

He nearly dropped the lantern he was carrying, but caught it in time and hurried to the door to chase the eyes away. They seemed to belong to a pack of children. They scattered in all directions as he opened the door, but then Mr Rummage heard a burst of laughter from the left, and looked along the front of the shop to see a group of idle good-for-nothing rascals hooting with laughter outside one of his windows.

How dare they! He gaped in amazement as they slapped their thighs, held their sides, bent double with merriment, pointing and making strange slapping movements with their hands.

'Constable! Constable!' he shouted, and set off at once to see what was the matter.

P.C. Jellicoe, who was built more for solidity than for speed, was getting fed up. This was the third time he'd had to come and sort out these customers of Mr Rummage's, and he had the rest of his beat to see to. He lumbered back and looked down at Mr Rummage disapprovingly.

'If you can't control your customers, Mr Rummage,' he said, 'I shall have to ask you to cover your windows up.'

'They're not my customers! I don't allow riff-raff like that into my emporium! While they're in the street they're the responsibility of the law, and I want them moved on, d'you hear?'

P.C. Jellicoe sniffed majestically, but since he couldn't think of anything to say in reply, he merely nodded austerely and sauntered along to the little crowd around the window.

From across the street, Benny and Thunderbolt and the twins, lurking in the shadows of Targett's Alley, watched in despair.

'Oy! Move along!' P.C. Jellicoe was saying. 'Clear the way there! You'll be facing a charge of obstruction if you don't move along!'

'But Constable, look at him!'

'It's as good as a play –'

'Move along!'

'But he's –'

'He's done it again! There he goes!'

'Cor, he nearly got it that time . . .'

All the spectators, in between their chortling, were swinging their arms about and slapping at the air. The constable raised his voice.

'This has the making of a scene of civil disobedience of the most reprehensible type. Be about your lawful business, else I shall be compelled to read the Riot Act and start making arrests.'

He was longing to look in the window and see what they were laughing at, but he feared that he might want to join in, which would be beneath his dignity.

If he had, he'd have seen Dippy still sitting on his chair, cured of his hiccups now but troubled by a wasp which had been slumbering in a dusty corner for months and had just woken up. It had taken a fancy to the pink of Dippy's cheeks, and kept trying to land there and see what they tasted like; and Dippy kept hearing it approach and swatting violently at the air, nearly losing his balance, and then trying to be still again.

When the onlookers had moved away, laughing and going *bzzz* at each other and slapping the air, P.C. Jellicoe finally turned to look in the window. By chance that coincided with a moment when the wasp was having a rest on the nose of one of the other dummies, and there was nothing moving but Dippy's eyes, swivelling wildly in their sockets because the wasp was just out of his line of sight and he had the uneasy feeling that it was walking down his neck.

P.C. Jellicoe saw Dippy's eyes move, and blinked and rubbed his own. But when he looked again the eyes were looking straight ahead – staring directly at him, in fact – and so unsettling was the effect of Dippy's disintegrating flour-caked cheeks and goggling bloodshot eyes that the constable took a step backwards in shock.

He hoped no one had seen him. He had half a mind to go and tell Mr Rummage to take the horrible thing out of the window as a danger to traffic. It was probably some new fashion, but if a nervous horse caught sight of it, it could easily cause an accident.

However, Mr Rummage had gone back into the shop, and the doors were locked. P.C. Jellicoe tested them all in order to look efficient, settled his helmet more firmly on his perspiring head, and strode off towards the Blackfriars Road at the regulation three miles an hour, leaving the road clear.

'Thank goodness for that!' breathed Benny. 'But what's that old clot Dippy up to?'

'I think he's signalling to us in semaphore,' said Thunderbolt. 'He's done X, and T, and Z, and F so far.'

'Well he can't spell then,' said Benny. 'I wish Rummage'd turn the bloomin' lights off. Then Dippy could slip out and open the doors. And where's Bridie? Seems to me you can't rely on anyone!'

As a matter of fact, Bridie was extremely busy. She and Sharky Bob were investigating the other mystery: that of the waxwork model that two lots of crooks, three if you counted the Frenchman, were after.

'What I reckon, Sharky,' she said, 'is that someone's got hold of this while Thunderbolt's back was turned, and hidden something in it.'

'Maybe dimonds,' he said.

'Yeah, could be. Cause it certainly ain't worth nothing on its own. So we oughter open it up, seems to me, and have a look.'

They were upstairs, having lugged the dummy up there for safety. The rest of the family were all crowded into the kitchen, where Uncle Paddy had the whistle going and Mr Sweeny was playing the fiddle, so for the moment the bedroom Bridie shared with five others was empty.

She set the candle-stump on the chest of drawers and hauled the dummy on the bed. It had got pretty battered in all its adventures, and it hadn't been beautiful to begin with, she had to admit.

'Take his clothes off,' said Sharky.

'Yeah, I'm going to. What's that ye're eating?'

'His ear,' said Sharky. 'It come off in me hand.'

'Well, what was yer hand doing on his ear in the first place?'

'Pulling it off,' he said. There was a grand simplicity about Sharky Bob.

'Oh, for goodness' sake . . . Eat it then. I don't suppose it'll do ye any harm, the amount of terrible rubbish ye've packed down yer manhole already. Now move back out the way. I'm going to try and get his clothes off without making them look any shabbier . . .'

84

Happily munching on the wax ear, Sharky sat on Siobhan's side of the mattress and watched Bridie wrestling with the dummy's clothes. She got them off eventually, and felt in the pockets, but the only thing there was a paper bag that had once contained boiled sweets. She gave it to Sharky to smell.

Then she felt along the coarse sacking sausage-shapes that were the dummy's arms and legs. In one leg she found a half-eaten turnip, and in the other she found a length of twine with an immense and complicated knot in it. She recognized it as the one Thunderbolt had used when he'd thought of taking up escapology. They'd spent forty minutes tying him up, and he'd taken three and a half hours to get loose; which, as Benny said, was a bit long to expect a music-hall audience to watch a kind of lump heaving and grunting. Thunderbolt had tired of escapology, and thrown the twine away, and here it was again. But not even Benny would imagine that gangs of crazed knot-fanciers would take desperate measures to steal it.

She threw the knotted twine into the corner and continued the surgery.

'Try his belly,' said Sharky Bob. 'I bet there's dimonds in his belly. That's where I'd put 'em, in the belly.'

'That's where you put everything, Sharky.'

'Yeah,' he said.

But the belly held only straw, and so did the chest and the arms. By the time she'd got to the neck, the bedroom was covered in wisps of hay and cornstalks and ragged bunches of straw and bits of sacking.

The head on its broomstick spine stared up reproach-
fully through its one remaining blood-alley eye.

Bridie scratched her own head and stared back
at it.

Then she plucked off the ear that Sharky hadn't
eaten and twisted it this way and that. It was funny
stuff; sort of sooty streaks in it; soft but not sticky;
and it did have a smell, or was she imagining it?

She sniffed at it. It did have a smell, and quite a
strong one, too, but it was nice. In fact it was very
nice. No wonder all those dogs had been so keen to
get at it. The more she rubbed it between her
fingers and thumb, the stronger and the nicer it
smelled.

'I wonder . . .' she said.

'It can't . . .' she went on.

'I don't suppose . . .' she muttered.

Then a light seemed to switch itself on in her
head. She slapped the ear back in place and clapped
her hands.

'Come on, Sharky!' she cried. 'I got it! I know
what they were after!'

And she thrust the head, horsehair whiskers and
blood-alley eye and all, into an old cotton shopping
bag and swept Sharky off the bed and down the
stairs.

Six

'It Screamed at Me!'

By this time, the kids in the alley opposite Rummage's were hopping with impatience. Dippy couldn't creep out while people were looking, and the window seemed to act as a magnet for all kinds of passers-by.

Including dogs. A suspicious-natured cur called Rags, who belonged to Fred Hipkiss the grocer, caught sight of Dippy's face as he stopped to investigate a lamppost. Rags suddenly leapt backwards, all his mangy hair stood on end, and a low growl came from his throat as he stalked up to the window. After his trouble with the hiccups and the wasp, Dippy was feeling rather sleepy, and gave a sudden jerk as he nearly nodded off. That roused Rag's fury. Clearly the horrible thing in there was challenging him to a fight. He leapt up at the window time and time again, barking madly, tumbling down each time only to get up in a frenzy of noise and temper and try again. Benny dealt with that; he ran across, lassoed Rags with Thunderbolt's emergency twine, and hauled him away.

The next problem was a young man called Ernest and his best girl, Ethel. They were strolling along moonily, stopping every so often to look at each other and sigh. Finally they drifted to a halt outside Dippy's window and gazed into each other's eyes.

The kids tiptoed across and hid in the angle of the bow window near by.

'Oh, Ernest,' Ethel sighed.

'Oh, Ethel,' Ernest mumbled.

'D'you love me, Ernest?'

'Oh, yes!'

'How much do you love me?'

'Oh . . . A *yuge* amount. Enormous.'

'Would you save me from a burning building?'

'Not half!'

'What else would you do for me, Ernest?'

'I'd . . .' Ernest paused.

'What?'

'Ethel, you see that dummy in the window?'

The gang froze. Ethel drew back her head from Ernest's shoulder.

'What about it?' she said.

'Well them gloves it's got on, they're just like the ones I told you about what I saw in Whiteley's.'

'Is that *all*? You're more interested in gloves than in me! I don't know why I bother with you – you don't love me at all!'

'I do! I do! Honest!'

'Well, what would you do for me?'

'I'd . . . I'd . . . Ethel, I'd swim the fiercest river in the world!'

'What else?'

'I'd . . . I'd run a thousand miles in me bare feet!'

'And?'

'I'd fight ten lions with me bare hands!'

'Oh, Ernest!' Ethel said softly. 'And when can I see you again?'

'Well, I'll come on Tuesday if it isn't raining,' he said.

'Ohhhh!'

And Ethel stamped her foot and flounced away. Ernest followed, protesting.

'Helpless!' said Angela. 'Run a thousand miles, fight ten lions –'

'And he'll come on Tuesday if it isn't raining. Huh!' Zerlina scoffed.

'Never mind them,' said Benny. 'What we gonna do about Dippy?'

'He's paralysed!' said Thunderbolt. 'It's that horse-reviver – it must've turned his blood to ice!'

'He's not moving at all!' said Benny. 'Wake up, you old clot!'

Dippy awoke with a loud snort. He blinked and looked around, and Benny tapped the glass again. Dippy peered forward and finally saw a row of desperate faces through the window. They were all saying something that he couldn't make out. Get to the floor? Give to the poor?

Then they started gestering at him. He thought they'd gone mad. He was about to say so to the man sitting next to him, when he had a horrible shock: *the man was dead!* Some horrible murder had been committed – a deranged taxidermist had stuffed the victim and sat him up in a chair – and he'd be next –

With a yelp of terror, Dippy tried to escape. He uncrossed his legs and stood up . . . But having been crossed for so long, the left one had gone to sleep, and when Dippy put his weight on it, it gave way.

'They've cut me leg off!' he gasped, grabbing at

90

the nearest thing, which happened to be one of the other two dummies left standing. It fell over with him, and the two of them landed locked in an embrace which made Dippy think of 'The Mummy's Vengeance', a story he'd read only the month before in one of Thunderbolt's penny shockers.

Incoherent with terror, he scrambled up, found the little door, wrenched it open, and tumbled through into the darkness of the shop, giving out little squeaks of fear.

The darkness was cool and quiet. Dippy still couldn't stand up straight, because his leg hadn't woken up. Maybe if he had just a little sip of the horse-reviver ... There was still a bit left in the flask.

He swallowed the last mouthful, smacking his lips with satisfaction.

Someone behind him was shouting. Wasn't it Benny's voice?

'Swallow some more!'

Or was it: 'Open the door?'

Yes! That was it! He had to open the door. Nothing to it, really ... He laughed a scornful laugh, thinking of how fearful he'd been.

Just get over the counter, and he could open the door and go home and have a lie-down, same as that other fellow was doing further along.

That other fellow was the 'Dux-Bak' Rainwear dummy which Mr Paget had put there earlier, but to Dippy's fuddled eyes it looked so comfortable lying there that he thought he'd join it. At the third try he got on to the polished mahogany counter, knocking off a display rack of 'Silk-O-Lene' cravats on the way, and stretched himself out peacefully. He fell asleep at once.

Meanwhile, alone in the basement, Mr Rummage was feverishly shovelling sixpences and shillings and half-crowns out of a tea-chest and into a Gladstone bag. Ever since he'd discovered the stash, hidden away under a trapdoor in the Ironmongery Department, he'd been torn between gloating over his good luck and trembling in case he was found out. And when he'd heard those two plain-clothes detectives this morning dropping hints that they were on to him, he'd been itching to get down here and dispose of the loot. If he could get the coins home to his comfortable house in Streatham, he could hide them there safely till the danger had passed.

He scooped up the last few sixpences with a 'Skoopitup' enamelled dustpan, shut the Gladstone bag with a snap and replaced the trapdoor. Then he hauled a heavy 'Skweezitout' mangle over to stand on top of it, looked around critically to make sure that he hadn't left any sixpences on the floor, and turned off the one hissing gaslight.

Nearly done, he thought. Soon be safe. He picked up the Gladstone bag, tiptoed to the stairs – and then froze.

Burglars!

There were noises from the floor above – muffled thuds and mutterings of a sort which wouldn't have been made by any honest person. Mr Rummage bit his lip. He wasn't afraid of burglars, but if he had to call a policeman while carrying a Gladstone bag full of snide coins . . .

Perhaps he could scare them away without involving the police.

Pausing only to take a 'Slysitoff' silver-plated carving knife from a nearby rack of kitchen equipment, he tiptoed up the stairs and into the main part of the shop.

Now, where had that noise come from?

He had the impression that it was somewhere in the direction of the Gentlemen's Outfitting Department.

Creeping through the dark, with his sinister black bag in one hand and the knife held high in the other, he made his evil way across the floor.

Meanwhile, in the street outside, the New Cut Gang were rapidly changing their plans.

'He's dead,' said Zerlina. 'That horse-reviver's done for him. He's only an old man.'

'I think he's fallen over and broken his leg,' said Thunderbolt. 'Or his neck, maybe.'

'Stuff!' said Angela. 'He's fast asleep. I can hear him snoring from out here!'

'Never mind all that,' said Benny impatiently. 'We got an emergency here. Oh no! There's Jellybelly . . .'

Just turning around the corner, under the flaring lights of the Theatre, P.C. Jellicoe was moving majestically into the New Cut.

But as the policeman stopped to inspect the pictures of the actresses outside the Theatre, Benny had an inspiration. He'd seen Thunderbolt fiddling absently with his lump of lead, and now Benny snatched it out of his hand and hurled it through the plate-glass window with an almighty crash. Glittering splinters of glass flew everywhere.

Before the others could react, Benny yelled, 'Mr Jellicoe! Mr Jellicoe! Quick!'

The constable had heard the noise and turned to look. When he saw Benny jumping and beckoning, he fumbled for his whistle.

'Hurry!' Benny yelled, and to the twins: 'Go and drag him – go on! Make him hurry –'

P.C. Jellicoe was breaking into a run, but he had to do it slowly by leaning forward and walking faster and faster. All the time he was trying to get his whistle to his mouth.

'Peep-peep!' came a feeble sound.

Thunderbolt ran to help. The constable lumbered up and stopped, heaving and puffing.

'Woss – goin' on? Eh? Oo – done – that?' he said, crimson and breathless, pointing at the window.

'Someone inside!' said Benny. 'We was just going past when there was this crash – someone's in there murdering people – look at the mess in the window!'

There was no denying that something awful *had* happened in that window. P.C. Jellicoe scratched his head.

'H'mm,' he said, still breathless. 'I better summon assistance.'

He felt for his whistle again, and turned towards the main entrance.

94

'Can I whistle for you, Mr Jellicoe?' said Thunderbolt. 'I reckon I got a bit more puff.'

'I think you're probably right,' said the policeman, and handed him the whistle before knocking loudly at the front door.

Thunderbolt filled his lungs and gave such a blast that it nearly shattered another window.

And that was the sound that did for Mr Rummage. By this time he'd crept into the Gentlemen's Outfitting Department. Hearing the smash of the window, he'd almost lost his temper: how dare they! Vandals! He took a tighter grip on the 'Slysitoff' carving knife. Any burglar he caught would be lucky to escape without a puncture.

And then came Thunderbolt's blast on the whistle.

Police!

He'd have to hide the coins. Quick! Where could he put them?

He looked around in a panic, and had an inspiration: the 'Dux-Bak' dummy on the counter! The one old Paget had knocked over! One quick slice with the carving knife and he could tip the coins into its belly and have done with them.

He scuttled over to the dummy and held the knife high . . .

And of course it wasn't that dummy at all. Dippy had been snoozing peacefully, stretched out on the counter, but when he heard footsteps he opened his eyes.

And seeing a wild-eyed lunatic about to slice him open with a carving knife, he sat up at once and screamed at the top of his voice.

Mr Rummage was even more startled, if possible. To find a dummy opening its hideous eyes and sitting up and screaming at him was more than his nerves could take.

He dropped the knife, leapt six feet backwards and four feet in the air, and screamed even louder. The Gladstone bag flew out of his hand and landed on the floor, where it burst open, scattering a fountain of coins everywhere.

And while Mr Rummage and Dippy were screaming at each other, the door burst open and in came P.C. Jellicoe, followed by a mob of howling children.

The shop was dark, of course, but Benny struck a match at once and lit the nearest gaslight.

'Look!' he said, pointing dramatically at the quivering Rummage. 'Guilt all over him, Mr Jellicoe!'

And holding the detective camera still, he took a photograph.

'Eh?' said the policeman. 'This is the shop-owner!'

'Look at these snide coins, Mr Jellicoe!' said Thunderbolt. 'Thousands of 'em! He's been uttering 'em! See? *He's* the one that did it!'

But all Mr Rummage was uttering now were the words 'The dummy – the dummy –' in a hoarse and broken voice. He pointed a quaking finger at the counter.

They all turned to look. There on the polished wood, lying full length, was a plaster dummy wearing a 'Dux-Bak' mackintosh.

P.C. Jellicoe strode up and prodded it with a mighty finger.

'Well?' he said. 'Wot about it?'

'It sat up! Its eyes! Its face! Horrible! It screamed at me!'

Under the other side of the counter, unseen by anyone, Angela clamped her hands over Dippy's mouth while Zerlina whispered in his ear 'Hush! Keep quiet, Dippy!'

Benny said loudly, 'It's clear what happened, Mr Jellicoe. Mr Rummage was going to hide all these snide coins what he's been passing out, and his guilty conscience got too much for him, and he had an illumination.'

'Hallucination,' said Thunderbolt.

'Yeah, one of them. You can tell he's had a shock. He musta been awful guilty. All them coins he's been passing out all this time . . .'

P.C. Jellicoe, still breathing heavily, turned over one of the sixpences in his fingers and then bit it.

'H'mm,' he said. 'Was this in your possession, Mr Rummage?'

'Yes. Yes. I admit it. It's true. I'm guilty. I confess. The dummy – don't make me stay with the dummy – take me away –'

P.C. Jellicoe pulled out his handcuffs.

'I have no alternative but to apply the full rigour of the law,' he said. 'Roger Rummage, I arrest you for the utterance of forged coins . . .'

In the excitement, the twins managed to smuggle Dippy out of the shop. A crowd was beginning to gather, and once they realized what Mr Rummage had been arrested for, they became quite angry.

'Rich man like him taking money out the pockets of the poor!'

'He should be ashamed!'

'Oughter cut his head off, I reckon. If it was good enough for King Charles, it's good enough for him.'

'All right, all right, move aside,' said P.C. Jellicoe, guarding the shivering shop-owner. 'This man is my lawful prisoner, and I'm a-going to take him down the nick and charge him according to due process of law, so clear out the way else I'll fetch you a belt round the ear.'

No one wanted to risk a belt round the ear from P.C. Jellicoe's ham-sized fists, so they made way, and a procession followed them all the way to the Police Station.

At the head of it was Thunderbolt.

'Mr Jellicoe, they'll have to release my Pa now, won't they? Cause if you've got the real criminal, they'll see Pa's not guilty.'

'I can't be answerable for the decisions of the magistrate,' said P.C. Jellicoe loftily.

And the gang had to put up with that. When they reached the Police Station the crowd was shut out, but Benny and Thunderbolt were admitted as witnesses.

The Sergeant on duty wrote down all the particulars, and looked very hard at Mr Rummage when he explained about the dummy.

'It sat up! It opened its eyes! It screamed at me! I can see now that it was a horrible warning, Sergeant. I should never have given in to temptation. I'll never do it again. Oh, those eyes! Those hideous eyes!'

'H'mm,' said the Sergeant, writing it all down.

And after Mr Rummage had been taken away to the cells, and the Gladstone bag and the coins and the 'Slysitoff' silver-plated carving knife had been locked away as evidence, the Sergeant looked up to find Thunderbolt still waiting anxiously at the desk.

'You still here? Wotcher want? There ain't no reward, you know.'

'I want my Pa,' Thunderbolt said.

'That's right!' said Benny. 'You can't hold two prisoners for the same offence. It's against the law. And you know old Rummage done it, cause he said so. *And* I got a photograph to prove it!'

He brandished the detective camera pugnaciously.

'So can I have my Pa back?' said Thunderbolt.

'No,' said the Sergeant.

The two boys opened their mouths and then shut them again. Thunderbolt suddenly felt very small.

'Why?' he said after a moment.

'Cause your Pa wasn't arrested for coining. He was arrested for another offence altogether, and he's been remanded on bail. Have you got fifty pounds to bail him out? I thought not. So what you going to do now?'

Seven

A Victim of the Spanish Inquisition

Thunderbolt just stood and gaped. Then he shut his mouth slowly and swallowed hard. Bail? Fifty *pounds*? And . . .

'What was he arrested for, then?' he said.

'Didn't they tell you, son?'

He could only shake his head. His heart was beating fast. The Sergeant was looking serious, and Thunderbolt could tell from his expression that he was about to say something terrible – but he didn't, because there was an interruption.

Someone was banging and shouting. A voice he recognized – Bridie's – was raised in anger, and when Bridie raised her voice, the whole street knew about it.

The Sergeant opened his mouth to protest, but another voice joined in. A foreign voice. A Frenchman's . . .

The Sergeant and the two boys all turned to look as the door burst open. P.C. Jellicoe, who'd been outside arguing, was nearly knocked to the ground as Bridie rushed in, with Sharky Bob at her heels, and the mysterious Frenchman only a foot or two behind.

Her face was as red as her hair, and a beam of triumph lit her up like a lighthouse. She forced her way to the counter and slammed down a cotton shopping bag.

'I done it!' she cried. 'I found him!'

'Woss all this?' said the Sergeant. 'Constable, what d'yer mean letting all this crew in?'

'She's got a . . . relic, Sarge,' said P.C. Jellicoe, looking pale and nervous.

'A *what*?'

'A . . . yuman 'ed,' gulped the constable.

Bridie scoffed, and opened the shopping bag to reveal the head of the waxwork Dippy. The Sergeant recoiled in horror.

'What in the world –'

'It's made o' wax, ye great baboon!' she cried. 'Except it *isn't* wax! Thunderbolt, it's all right! Ye're rich, old feller! Tell him, Sharky!'

'It's *amblegrease*!' shouted Sharky Bob, joining in as Bridie whirled Thunderbolt in a jig.

And suddenly everyone was talking at once, including the Frenchman. But no one's voice was louder than Thunderbolt's, as he shouted:

'SHUT UP!'

'Just what I was about to say,' said the Sergeant. 'You, girl, what's-yer-name, *you* talk. No one else.'

So Bridie breathlessly said, 'It was all them fellers trying to steal our waxwork. And Monsewer here, I didn't think he was a thief, but we never let him talk. And it got me thinking, and me and Sharky opened up the dummy and found nothing bar straw and old bits o' rubbish, so it had to be the head, ye see? And it was Thunderbolt's lump of wax! *Except* that I remembered his homework . . .'

And she spread out a filthy piece of paper on the counter. The Sergeant read:

'*Ambergris: fatty substance of a marmoriform or striated appearance, exuded from the intestines of the sperm whale, and highly esteemed by perfumiers ...* What the blazes does that mean? Striated? Marmoriform?'

'Dunno,' said Benny. 'No one's gonna know till we get to S and M in the dictionary. We're only on A.'

'That's not important,' said Bridie impatiently. 'It's the perfume bit that matters. So I found Monsewer here, cause I reckoned that's what he was after, and I was right! I was *right*!'

The little Frenchman, who had been twitching with excitement, said, 'Yes! Mademoiselle is correct! I am Gaston Leroux, *parfumier*! I am the maker of the finest, the most exquisite perfumes and scents in the weurld! And when my *neuhse* – this organ so delicate and senstive –' He touched his nose with the fingertips of both hands, as if he was making sure it was stuck on properly – 'when my highly-trained and irreplaceable *neuhse* caught the fragrance of ambergris, I followed it. Then I lost it. Then it followed *me*. This is the finest – the most profoundly beautiful piece of ambergris I have evair seen! I *meust* have it! My genius demands it!'

The Sergeant rubbed his eyes.

'What d'you mean, you must have it? It belongs to young Thunderbolt here, by the look of things. If you want it, you'll have to buy it off him. What's it worth? A couple of quid?'

'More'n that!' said Bridie. 'Tell 'em, Monsewer! Go on!'

'Ah weel peh,' said M. Leroux with dignity, 'the market prahce for this. And that is six pounds per ounce.'

No one spoke. No one moved. No one could.

Finally Thunderbolt uttered a squeak.

'Six *pounds*? An *ounce*? But there must be . . .'

He goggled at the battered head, with its horsehair moustache, its blood-alley eye, its cracked and stained teeth. Then the Sergeant blew out his cheeks.

'Where's them postal scales?' he said. 'Look sharp, Constable!'

P.C. Jellicoe handed him a little brass set of scales from the desk.

'I don't weunt the moustache,' said M. Leroux. 'Or the eye. Or those teeth. Ugh! Remove them!'

Benny dug them out, and the Sergeant tenderly lifted the head on to the scales and balanced it with the little brass weights.

'I make that four pounds, fourteen and a half ounces,' the Sergeant said. 'That correct, Monsewer?'

'Perfectly!'

Out came a notebook. The Sergeant licked the point of his pencil and began to work out the sum, and so did M. Leroux, and so did P.C. Jellicoe. The constable gave up after a minute and waited for the other two to finish. Finally the Sergeant showed his sum to M. Leroux, and they nodded.

'Four hundred and seventy-one pounds,' said the Sergeant.

'Absolutely correct,' said M. Leroux.

'But . . . Sharky must've ate about fifty quid's worth!' said Benny, overawed. 'And old Ron the terrier – he ate the nose –'

And they all looked at Thunderbolt. First he went bright red, then he went pale, then he sniffed very hard and said, 'Well . . . Blimey. That's . . . That's enough to pay Pa's bail! I can get him out!'

'He's a lucky man,' said the Sergeant.

M. Leroux paid some gold on account, and the Sergeant offered to put the head in the safe until the cheque had cleared, so that everything was above board, and then P.C. Jellicoe took Thunderbolt along to the magistrate's to see about the bail. Thunderbolt was feeling so dizzy he could hardly think.

When the magistrate heard what it was about he said, 'Oh dear me, Mr Dobney, yes, I remember the case . . . Dear dear! Out at last, is he? Bright spark, that fellow! Shocking case! Ha ha ha!'

Thunderbolt didn't understand it at all, and he was far too nervous to ask. Then there came another walk, to the prison in Renfrew Road, down past Bedlam where the poor lunatics were locked up.

P.C. Jellicoe saw Thunderbolt looking up at the great dark bulk of the hospital.

'Pity the poor fellers in there,' he said. 'Take more'n amblegrease to get *them* out.'

The Prison Governor took the magistrate's order and sent for a warder, who left the room jingling a bunch of keys. And much sooner than Thunderbolt had expected, there was Pa, in prison overalls, blinking and rubbing his hair. The Governor left them alone for a minute, and neither Thunderbolt nor Pa knew what to say.

Then Pa put his arms out, and Thunderbolt hurled himself at Pa and pressed his wet cheeks against his father's chest, squeezing him round the middle tight enough to hurt. He felt he was hurting both of them: himself for ever thinking that his dear Pa could do anything as mean as forge money, and Pa for not telling him what he *was* doing, and himself again for being afraid to go to the police because of that silly lump of lead.

His father patted his shoulder over and over again, and ruffled his hair.

''S all right, old son,' he said. 'I'm free now. We'll get out in a minute and go home. Cor, I'm starving. They give us gruel in this place what tastes like wallpaper paste. And *you* ain't et for days, by the look of yer.'

'Mrs Malone's been looking after me,' said Thunderbolt, his face still muffled in Pa's chest. Then he let go, and while Pa got his proper clothes on, Thunderbolt blew his nose and wiped his eyes so they could both pretend he hadn't been crying.

They said goodbye to P.C. Jellicoe, and good riddance to the prison, and strolled along the midnight streets towards home. There was a coffee stall in St George's Circus, outside the Surrey Theatre, and they stopped and had a cup of coffee with two toffs in top hats, one sailor who was lost, and two brightly-painted young ladies.

'This is my son,' Pa announced. 'He's just sprung me out o' captivity. And in honour of my release,

I'm going to stand coffee all round. Serve it up, my man, and raise your cups, ladies and gentlemen, in a toast to my son Thunderbolt.'

The toffs and the sailor and the young ladies all drank Thunderbolt's health, and he felt as proud as the Prince of Wales.

Later, when they'd got home and locked the door and lit the fire to make some cocoa on, and Thunderbolt had told Pa all about the ambergris, he asked what he'd wanted to ask ever since the whole business began.

'Pa,' he said, 'what *did* they lock you up for? Was it to do with them batteries in the basement?'

'Yeah,' Pa said.

'Well . . .' Thunderbolt went on. 'What were you doing?'

Pa twisted his mouth under his moustache. Then he rubbed his hair again so it stuck out in all directions.

'It's a bit embarrassing,' he said. 'I didn't know how to tell yer, cause you might think . . . I dunno what you might've thought. It was electric ladies' corsets.'

'*What?*'

'Electric corsets for ladies with backache. See, I had this notion of a corset with wires in it, and a battery, and you could regulate – well, I don't mean *you*, I mean the lady – she could turn the current up or down and keep herself warm and ease the backache. Only the first ladies what tried 'em kept getting awful shocks, and it was costing me more and more to insulate it proper . . .'

He had to stop because he was smiling, and so was Thunderbolt, and then the thought of electrically heated ladies leaping in alarm with sparks flying out of their corsets was too much for them, and they burst out laughing.

'So I borrowed some money to cover it, and I couldn't pay it back . . .' said Pa eventually, wiping his eyes. 'Fizz! Crack! Hop!'

And that sent Thunderbolt off again. He kept waking up in the night and finding a broad grin on his face, so he knew he must be happy.

But the gang still had some unfinished business to attend to, and no one was more aware of it than Benny.

'We promised Dippy,' he said. 'We *promised* the old boy we'd get him in the Waxworks, and we ain't. Here! When's Monsewer coming back for the rest of the head?'

'This afternoon,' said Thunderbolt. 'The money's cleared all right now, so the Sergeant said he could have it any time he likes, and he's going to fetch it at three o'clock, he says.'

'Right,' said Benny. 'You leave it to me.'

And whatever Benny said to M. Leroux must have worked, because when the others came out of school that afternoon, Benny met them by the sweet-shop, smiling proudly.

'Follow me,' he said, and led them round the corner to the Waxwork Museum.

Professor Dupont the proprietor welcomed them, to everyone's surprise, and showed them into his office, which was lined with shelves containing rows and rows of wax heads.

'Well, ladies and gentlemen,' said the Professor, 'my eminent compatriot M. Leroux has told me of the gallant deeds of our friend M. Hisspot.'

'Hitchcock,' said Bridie.

'Exactly. Well, in view of his great fame and valour, I am prepared to exhibit a figure of M. Twitchlock.'

'Hitchcock!'

'Just as you say. M. Leroux showed me the head you made, and I must say I revised my opinion of your skill. In fact I have never seen so remarkable a work of art before.'

Benny was glowing with modesty. 'Yeah,' he said. 'I reckon I could do anyone. I could do Sexton Blake for yer –'

'We will stick to M. Fishdock for now,' said the Professor. 'What colour are his eyes?'

He opened a drawer full of eyes, and while the gang argued about the precise colour of Dippy's, the Professor took a second-hand head from the shelf.

'Take this wax,' he said, 'and make me a portrait of M. Hitchpot, and I will give it a place of honour in the Museum.'

So they took the head, and they chose some eyes, and they set to work.

Actually, of course, it was Benny who did the sculpting. He felt he had to redeem himself, because the picture in the detective camera, when it was developed, showed nothing but a murky glimpse of Benny's own stomach; he'd had it on back to front.

Still, that didn't matter, as Mr Rummage had confessed.

So he got to work, and life got back to normal. The twins were busy getting racing tips from the stable-boys in Hodgkins's Livery Stables, and Thunderbolt had to catch up with his homework. They'd got to C now: cataplasm, châtelaine, cochineal ... As for Bridie, she'd fallen in love with Edmund Fitzwilkins, an actor at the Surrey Theatre, and she hung around the stage door, weak with longing.

Pa paid back the money he'd borrowed, and the magistrates let him off with a caution, once they managed to keep their faces straight enough to do so.

'No more electric corsets,' they said. 'Shocking idea.'

'Wouldn't dream of it,' said Pa.

So Benny worked alone; but being a genius, he didn't mind that. The others got hold of Dippy from time to time and dragged him to the hideout to model. He still felt a bit odd from the effects of the horse-reviver, but he didn't want to refuse in case they made him do something else dangerous.

And after three days of concentrated work, the head was ready. Benny unveiled it proudly, and Dippy and the others stood around, dumb with admiration, almost.

'It's as good as the first one,' said Zerlina.

'It's better,' said Angela. 'More *passionate*.'

'It's a masterpiece,' said Thunderbolt. 'It's revolutionary!'

As for Dippy, all he could say was, 'Thank you, kids. Thank you. I can't hardly believe it . . .'

The Professor took it in with delight.

'Formidable!' he said. 'I shall do my best to provide a body worthy of this – this masterpiece! Truly it displays an imaginative vision the equal of Edgar Allan Peuhh . . . Leave it with me, dear boy! I shall make it the centrepiece of a display that will astonish the weurld! Come back on Saturday for the grand opening.'

So they did. Dippy went with them, naturally, with his best schmutter on and his hair stuck down with macassar oil. He looked a treat. Mr Dobney came too. There was a big crowd, thronging the Museum for a sight of the startling new exhibit. There were posters about it:

SEE THE ASTONISHING NEW FIGURE!
Sculpted by an Eminent Local Artist
and modelled by a citizen of Lambeth,
MR HICKY DIPSTOCK,
the figure
BREAKS ALL BARRIERS
of expressive realism, and
SETS NEW STANDARDS
OF ARTISTIC ASTONISHMENT.
IN THE BASEMENT NOW!

'The basement?' said Benny. 'That's the Chamber of Horrors, innit?'

They hurried down the dark narrow stairs and into the dimly lit, brick-vaulted, cobwebbed dungeon that housed the worst horrors the Wax Museum offered. A notice said:

> **A PRIZE OF £5 WILL BE OFFERED TO ANYONE WHO CAN STAY IN THE CHAMBER OF HORRORS OVERNIGHT!**

and underneath was added:

> **IN VIEW OF THE POWER AND GRUESOMENESS OF THE NEW DISPLAY, THE PRIZE IS RAISED TO £10!**

The gang's eyes swept over the scenes of murder and carnage that lined the walls – throats being cut, heads being chopped off – they'd seen it all before. But in one corner an excited crowd was buzzing with chatter, and as the kids looked, two people had to be helped away pale and shaking.

'Where is it?' said Benny. 'What've they done with my masterpiece?'

He shoved his way through the crowd, the others close behind. Then they stopped by a sign that said:

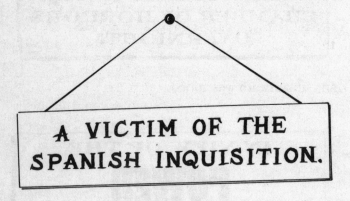

A VICTIM OF THE SPANISH INQUISITION.

Lit by a flickering torch was a scene from a dungeon: a priest, a black-masked torturer wielding a red-hot pair of tongs, and cowering on the floor in rags, a poor shivering figure with the head of Dippy Hitchcock, as modelled by the eminent local artist Mr Benny Kaminsky.

It was exactly as Benny had made it. Not a bit had been changed, but somehow, in these surroundings, it expressed a hideous, nameless fear, enough to give anyone nightmares. The rolling eyes – the lips drawn back in a cry of anguish – every line of the poor tormented face spoke of despair and horror.

'H'mm,' said Benny. 'It never looked like that in the hideout.'

'It's good though, Dippy,' said Mr Dobney.

And the people around seemed to agree.

'Look at the suffering in his eyes!'

'I can't bear to look at it . . .'

'They must've done things to him what was too horrible to contemplate!'

'He must of been through mortal agony . . .'

And that, thought Dippy, was not very far from the truth.

ww.puffin.co.uk.www.puffin.co.uk.www.puffin.co.uk
okinfo.competitions.news.games.sneakpreviews
ww.puffin.co.uk.www.puffin.co.uk.www.puffin.co.uk
dventure.bestsellers.fun.coollinks.freestuff
ww.puffin.co.uk.www.puffin.co.uk.www.puffin.co.uk
xplore.yourshout.awards.toptips.authorinfo
ww.puffin.co.uk.www.puffin.co.uk.www.puffin.co.uk
eatbooks.greatbooks.greatbooks.greatbooks
ww.puffin.co.uk.www.puffin.co.uk.www.puffin.co.uk
views.poems.jokes.authorevents.audioclips
ww.puffin.co.uk.www.p   co.uk.www.puffin.co.uk
terviews.e-mailupdates.bookinfo.competitions.news

www.puffin.co.uk

ames.sneakpreviews.adventure.bestsellers.fun
ww.puffin.co.uk.www.puffin.co.uk.www.puffin.co.uk
ookinfo.competitions.news.games.sneakpreviews
ww.puffin.co.uk.www.puffin.co.uk.www.puffin.co.uk
dventure.bestsellers.fun.coollinks.freestuff
ww.puffin.co.uk.www.puffin.co.uk.www.puffin.co.uk
xplore.yourshout.awards.toptips.authorinfo
ww.puffin.co.uk.www.puffin.co.uk.www.puffin.co.uk
eatbooks.greatbooks.greatbooks.greatbooks
ww.puffin.co.uk.www.puffin.co.uk.www.puffin.co.uk
views.poems.jokes.authorevents.audioclips
ww.puffin.co.uk.www.puffin.co.uk.www.puffin.co.uk

Choosing a brilliant book
can be a tricky business...
but not any more

www.puffin.co.uk

The best selection of books at your fingertips

So get clicking!

Searching the site is easy – you'll find
what you're looking for at the click of a mouse,
from great authors to brilliant books and more!

Everyone's got different taste . . .

I like stories that make me laugh

Animal stories are definitely my favourite

I'd say fantasy is the best

I like a bit of romance

It's got to be adventure for me

I really love poetry

I like a good mystery

Whatever you're into, we've got it covered . . .

www.puffin.co.uk

Psst!
What's happening?

sneakpreviews@puffin

For all the inside information on the hottest new books,

click on the Puffin

www.puffin.co.uk

hotnews@puffin

Hot off the press!
You'll find all the latest exclusive Puffin news here

Where's it happening?
Check out our author tours and events programme

Best-sellers
What's hot and what's not? Find out in our charts

E-mail updates
Sign up to receive all the latest news
straight to your e-mail box

Links to the coolest sites
Get connected to all the best author web sites

Book of the Month
Check out our recommended reads

www.puffin.co.uk

Read more in Puffin

For complete information about books available from Puffin – and Penguin – and how to order them, contact us at the appropriate address below. Please note that for copyright reasons the selection of books varies from country to country.

www.puffin.co.uk

In the United Kingdom: Please write to Dept EP, Penguin Books Ltd, Bath Road, Harmondsworth, West Drayton, Middlesex UB7 ODA

In the United States: Please write to Penguin Putnam Inc., P.O. Box 12289, Dept B, Newark, New Jersey 07101–5289 or call 1–800–788–6262

In Canada: Please write to Penguin Books Canada Ltd, 10 Alcorn Avenue, Suite 300, Toronto, Ontario M4V 3B2

In Australia: Please write to Penguin Books Australia Ltd, P.O. Box 257, Ringwood, Victoria 3134

In New Zealand: Please write to Penguin Books (NZ) Ltd, Private Bag 102902, North Shore Mail Centre, Auckland 10

In India: Please write to Penguin Books India Pvt Ltd, 11 Panscheel Shopping Centre, Panscheel Park, New Delhi 110 017

In the Netherlands: Please write to Penguin Books Netherlands bv, Postbus 3507, NL–1001 AH Amsterdam

In Germany: Please write to Penguin Books Deutschland GmbH, Metzlerstrasse 26, 60594 Frankfurt am Main

In Spain: Please write to Penguin Books S. A., Bravo Murillo 19, 1° B, 28015 Madrid

In Italy: Please write to Penguin Italia s.r.l., Via Felice Casati 20, I–20124 Milano

In France: Please write to Penguin France S. A., 17 rue Lejeune, F–31000 Toulouse

In Japan: Please write to Penguin Books Japan, Ishikiribashi Building, 2–5–4, Suido, Bunkyo-ku, Tokyo 112

In South Africa: Please write to Longman Penguin Southern Africa (Pty) Ltd, Private Bag X08, Bertsham 2013